THE CASE
OF THE
MISSING MARQUESS

THE CASE
OF THE
MISSING MARQUESS

AN ENOLA HOLMES MYSTERY

NANCY SPRINGER

SCHOLASTIC INC.

New York Toronto London Auckland Sydney
Mexico City New Delhi Hong Kong Buenos Aires

To my mother — N. S.

ISBN-13: 978-0-439-92937-0
ISBN-10: 0-439-92937-7

12 11 10 9 8 7 6 5 4 3 2 1   7 8 9 10 11 12/0

Printed in the U.S.A.   40

First Scholastic printing, March 2007

Design by Marikka Tamura

In the East End of London After Dark, August, 1888

THE ONLY LIGHT STRUGGLES FROM THE FEW gas street-lamps that remain unbroken, and from pots of fire suspended above the cobblestones, tended by old men selling boiled sea snails outside the public houses. The stranger, all dressed in black from her hat to her boots, slips from shadow to shadow as if she were no more than a shadow herself, unnoticed. Where she comes from, it is unthinkable for a female to venture out at night without the escort of a husband, father, or brother. But she will do whatever she must in order to search for the one who is lost.

Wide-eyed beneath her black veil, she scans, seeks, watches as she walks. She sees broken glass on the cracked pavements. She sees rats boldly walking about, trailing their disgusting hairless tails.

1

She sees ragged children running barefoot amid the rats and the broken glass. She sees couples, men in red flannel vests and women in cheap straw bonnets, reeling along arm in arm. She sees someone lying along a wall, drunk or asleep amid the rats or maybe even dead.

Looking, she also listens. Somewhere a hurdy-gurdy spews a jingle into the sooty air. The black-veiled seeker hears that tipsy music. She hears a little girl calling, "Daddy? Da?" outside the door of a pub. She hears screams, laughter, drunken cries, street vendors calling, "Oysters! Sauce 'em in winegar and swaller 'em whole, fat 'uns four fer a penny!"

She smells the vinegar. She smells gin, boiled cabbage, and hot sausage, the salty waft of the nearby harbour, and the stench of the river Thames. She smells rotting fish. She smells raw sewage.

She quickens her pace. She must keep moving, for not only is she a seeker, but she is sought. The black-veiled hunter is hunted. She must walk far so that the men who are pursuing her cannot find her.

At the next street-lamp, she sees a woman with painted lips and smudged eyes waiting in a doorway. A hansom cab drives up, stops, and a man in a tail coat and a shining silk top-hat gets out. Even though the woman in the doorway wears a low-cut evening gown that might once have belonged to a lady of the gentleman's social class, the black-clad watcher does not think the gentleman is here to go dancing. She sees the prostitute's haggard eyes, haunted with fear no matter how much her red-smeared lips smile. One like her was recently found dead a few streets away, slit wide open. Averting her gaze, the searcher in black walks on.

An unshaven man lounging against a wall winks at her. "Missus, what yer doing all alone? Don't yer want some company?" If he were a gentleman, he would not have spoken to her without being intro-duced. Ignoring him, she hastens past. She must speak to no one. She does not belong here. The knowledge does not trouble her, for she has never belonged anywhere. And in a sense she has always been alone. But her heart is not without pain as she scans the shadows, for she has no home now, she is a stranger in the world's largest city, and she does not know where she will lay her head tonight.

And if, Lord willing, she lives until morning, she

can only hope to find the loved one for whom she is searching.

Deeper and deeper into shadows and East London dockside slums, she walks on. Alone.

CHAPTER
THE
FIRST

I WOULD VERY MUCH LIKE TO KNOW WHY my mother named me "Enola," which, backwards, spells *alone*. Mum was, or perhaps still is, fond of ciphers, and she must have had something in mind, whether foreboding or a sort of left-handed blessing or, already, plans, even though my father had not yet passed away.

In any event, "You will do very well on your own, Enola," she would tell me nearly every day as I was growing up. Indeed, this was her usual absent-minded farewell as she went off with sketch-book, brushes, and watercolours to roam the countryside. And indeed, alone was very much how she left me when, on the July evening of my fourteenth birthday, she neglected to return to Ferndell Hall, our home.

As I had my celebration anyway, with Lane the butler and his wife the cook, the absence of my mother did not at first trouble me. Although cordial enough when we met, Mum and I seldom interfered in one another's concerns. I assumed that some urgent business kept her elsewhere, especially as she had instructed Mrs. Lane to give me certain parcels at tea-time.

Mum's gifts to me consisted of

a drawing kit: paper, lead pencils, a penknife for sharpening them, and India-rubber erasers, all cleverly arranged in a flat wooden box that opened into an easel;

a stout book entitled *The Meanings of Flowers: Including Also Notes Upon the Messages Conveyed by Fans, Handkerchiefs, Sealing-Wax, and Postage-Stamps;*

a much smaller booklet of ciphers.

While I could draw only to a limited degree, Mother encouraged the small knack I had. She knew I enjoyed my sketching, as I enjoyed reading almost any book, on whatever topic—but as for ciphers, she knew I did *not* much care for them. Nevertheless, she had made this little book for me with her own hands, as I could plainly see, folding and stitching together pages she had decorated with dainty watercolour flowers.

Obviously she had been at work on this gift for some time. She did not lack thought for me, I told myself. Firmly. Several times throughout the evening.

While I had no idea where Mum might be, I expected she would either come home or send a message during the night. I slept peacefully enough.

However, the next morning, Lane shook his head. No, the lady of the house had not returned. No, there had been no word from her.

Outside, grey rain fell, fitting my mood, which grew more and more uneasy.

After breakfast, I trotted back upstairs to my bedroom, a pleasant refuge where the wardrobe, washstand, dresser, and so forth were painted white with pink-and-blue stencilled posies around the edges. "Cottage furniture," folk called it, cheap stuff suitable only for a child, but I liked it. Most days.

Not today.

I could not have stayed indoors; indeed, I could not sit down except hastily, to pull galoshes over my boots. I wore shirt and knickerbockers, comfortable clothing that had previously belonged to my older brothers, and over these I threw a waterproof. All rubbery, I thumped downstairs and took an umbrella from the stand in the hallway. Then I exited through the kitchen, telling Mrs. Lane, "I am going to have a look around."

Odd; these were the same words I said nearly every day when I went out to—look for things, though generally I didn't know what. Anything. I would climb trees just to see what might be there: snail shells with bands of maroon and yellow, nut clusters, birds' nests. And if I found a magpie's nest, I would look for things in it: shoe buttons, bits of shiny ribbon, somebody's lost earring. I would pretend that something of great value was lost, and I was searching—

Only this time I was not pretending.

Mrs. Lane, too, knew it was different this time. She should have called, "Where's your hat, Miss Enola?" for I never wore one. But she said nothing as she watched me go.

Go to have a look around for my mother.

I really thought I could find her myself.

Once out of sight of the kitchen, I began running back and forth like a beagle, hunting for any sign of Mum. Yesterday morning, as a birthday treat, I had been allowed to lie abed; therefore I had not seen my mother go out. But assuming that she had, as usual, spent some hours drawing studies of flowers and plants, I looked for her first on the grounds of Ferndell.

Managing her estate, Mum liked to let growing things alone. I rambled through flower gardens run wild, lawns invaded by gorse and brambles, forest shrouded in grape and ivy vines. And all the while the grey sky wept rain on me.

The old collie dog, Reginald, trotted along with me until he grew tired of getting wet, then left to find shelter. Sensible creature. Soaked to my knees, I knew I should do likewise, but I could not. My anxiety had accelerated, along with my gait, until now terror drove me like a lash. Terror that my mother lay out here somewhere, hurt or sick or—a fear I could not entirely deny, as Mum was far from young—she might have been struck down by heart failure. She might be—but one could not even think it so baldly; there were other words. Expired. Crossed over. Passed away. Gone to join my father.

No. Please.

One would think that, as Mother and I were not "close," I should not have minded her disappearance very much. But quite the contrary; I felt dreadful, because it seemed all my fault if anything had gone badly with her. Always I felt to blame for—for whatever, for breathing—because I had been born indecently late in Mother's life, a scandal, a burden, you see. And always I had counted upon setting things right after I was grown. Someday, I hoped, somehow, I would make of my life a shining light that would lift me out of the shadow of disgrace.

And then, you understand, my mother would love me.

So she had to be alive.

And I *must* find her.

Searching, I crisscrossed forest where generations of squires had hunted hares and grouse; I climbed down and up the shelving, fern-draped rock of the grotto for which the estate was named—a place I loved, but today I did not linger. I continued to the edge of the park, where the woods ended and the farmland began.

And I searched onward into the fields, for Mum may very well have gone there, for the sake of the flowers. Being not too far from the city, Ferndell tenants had taken to farming bluebells and pansies and lilies instead of vegetables, as they could better prosper by delivering fresh blossoms daily to Covent Garden. Here grew rows of roses, crops of coreopsis, flaming patches of zinnias and poppies, all for London. Looking on the fields of flowers, I dreamt of a bright city where every day smiling maids placed fresh bouquets in every chamber of the mansions, where every evening gentlewomen and royal ladies decked and scented themselves, their hair and gowns, with anemones and violets. London, where—

But today the acres of flowers hung sodden with rain, and my dreams of London lasted only a breath or two before evaporating like the mist steaming up from the fields. Vast fields. Miles of fields.

Where was Mother?

In my dreams, you see—my Mum dreams, not the London ones—I would find her myself, I would be a heroine, she would gaze up at me in gratitude and adoration when I rescued her.

But those were dreams and I was a fool.

So far I had searched only a quarter of the estate, much less the farmlands. If Mum lay injured, she'd give up the ghost before I could find her all by myself.

Turning, I hurried back to the hall.

There, Lane and Mrs. Lane swooped upon me like a pair of turtledoves upon the nest, he plucking sopping coat and umbrella and boots from me, she hustling me towards the kitchen to get warm. While it was not her place to scold me, she made her views plain. "A person would have to be simpleminded to stay out in the rain for hours on end," she told the big coal-burning stove as she levered one of its lids off. "Don't matter whether a person is common or aristocrat, if a person catches a chill, it could kill her." This to the teakettle she was placing on the stove. "Consumption is no respecter of persons or circumstances." To the tea canister. There was no need for me to respond, for she wasn't talking to me. She would not have been permitted to say anything of the sort *to* me. "It's all very well for a person to be of an independent mind without going looking for quinsy or pleurisy or pneumonia or worse." To the teacups. Then she turned to face me, and her tone also about-faced. "Begging your pardon, Miss

Enola, will you take luncheon? Won't you draw your chair closer to the stove?"

"I'll brown like toast if I do. No, I do not require luncheon. Has there been any word of Mother?" Although I already knew the answer—for Lane or Mrs. Lane would have told me at once if they had heard anything—still, I could not help asking.

"Nothing, miss." She swaddled her hands in her apron as if wrapping a baby.

I stood. "Then there are some notes I must write."

"Miss Enola, there's no fire in the library. Let me bring the things to you here at the table, miss."

I felt just as glad not to have to sit in the great leather chair in that gloomy room. Into the warm kitchen Mrs. Lane fetched paper imprinted with our family crest, the ink pot and the fountain pen from the library desk, along with some blotting paper.

Dipping the pen into the ink, on the cream-coloured stationery I wrote a few words to the local constabulary, informing them that my mother seemed to have gone astray and requesting them to kindly organise a search for her.

Then I sat thinking: Did I really have to?

Unfortunately, yes. I could put it off no longer.

More slowly I wrote another note, one that would soon wing for miles via wire to be printed out by a teletype machine as:

LADY EUDORIA VERNET HOLMES MISSING SINCE YESTERDAY
STOP PLEASE ADVISE STOP ENOLA HOLMES

I directed this wire to Mycroft Holmes, of Pall Mall, in London.

And also, the same message, to Sherlock Holmes, of Baker Street, also in London.

My brothers.

CHAPTER THE SECOND

AFTER SIPPING THE TEA URGED UPON ME by Mrs. Lane, I changed to dry knickerbockers and started off to deliver my notes to the village.

"But the rain—the wet—Dick will take them," Mrs. Lane offered, wringing her hands in her apron again.

Her grown son, she meant, who did odd jobs around the estate, while Reginald, the somewhat more intelligent collie dog, supervised him. Rather than tell Mrs. Lane I did not trust Dick with this important errand, I said, "I shall make some inquiries while I'm there. I will take the bicycle."

This was not some old high-wheeled boneshaker, but an up-to-date "dwarf" bicycle with pneumatic tyres, perfectly safe.

Pedalling through the drizzle, I stopped for a

moment at the lodge — Ferndell is small for a hall, really only a stone house with its chest puffed out, so to speak, but it needs must have a drive, a gate, and therefore a lodge.

"Cooper," I asked the lodge-keeper, "would you open the gate for me? And by the way, do you happen to recall opening it for my mother yesterday?"

To which, not quite masking his astonishment at such a question, he replied in the negative. At no time had Lady Eudoria Holmes passed this way.

After he had let me out, I pedalled the short distance to Kineford village.

At the post office I sent my telegrams. Then I left off my note at the constabulary, and spoke with the officer, before I began my rounds. I stopped at the vicarage, the greengrocer's, the bakery, the confectionery, the butcher's shop, the fishmonger's, and so forth, inquiring after my mother as discreetly as I could. No one had seen her. The vicar's wife, among others, raised her eyebrows at me. I supposed it was because of my knickerbockers. For public cycling, you see, I should have been wearing "rationals" — bloomers covered by a waterproof skirt — or indeed any kind of skirt long enough to conceal my ankles.

I knew my mother was criticised for failing properly to drape vulgar surfaces such as coal scuttles, the back of her piano, and me.

Shocking child that I was.

I never questioned my disgrace, for to do so would have been to broach matters of which a "nice" girl must remain ignorant. I had observed, however, that most married women disappeared into the house every year or two, emerging several months later with a new child, to the number of perhaps a dozen, until they either ceased or expired. My mother, by comparison, had produced only my two much older brothers. Somehow this prior restraint made my late arrival all the more shameful for a gentleman Rationalist logician and his well-bred artistic wife.

The eyebrow-raisers bent their heads together and whispered as I pedalled around Kineford again, this time inquiring at the inn, the smithy, the tobacconist's, and the public house, places where "nice" females seldom set foot.

I learned nothing.

And despite my best smiles and by-the-way manner, I could almost hear a crescendo of excited gossip, conjecture, and rumour rising behind me as I returned to Ferndell Hall in an unhappy state of mind.

"No one has seen her," I answered Mrs. Lane's mute, questioning glance, "or has any idea where she might be."

Again waving aside her offers of luncheon— although now it was nearly tea-time—I trudged up-stairs to my mother's suite of rooms and stood outside the hallway door, considering. Mum kept her door locked. To spare Mrs. Lane the trouble, supposedly—for Lane and Mrs. Lane were the only house-servants—Mum cleaned her rooms herself. She hardly ever allowed anyone to enter, but under the circumstances . . .

I decided to go ahead.

Laying my hand upon the doorknob, I fully ex-pected I would have to hunt up Lane to get the key.

But the knob turned in my grasp.

The door opened.

And I knew in that moment, if I had not known before, that everything had changed.

Looking about me in the hush of my mother's sitting room, I felt rather more worshipful than if I were in a chapel. I had read Father's logic books, you see, and Malthus, and Darwin; like my parents I held rational and scientific views—but being in Mum's room made me feel as if I wanted to believe. In something. The soul, perhaps, or the spirit.

Mum had made this room a sanctuary of the artistic spirit. Panels of Japanese lotus-patterned silk dressed the windows, drawn back to let in the light upon slender furnishings of maple wood carved to resemble bamboo, very different from the hulking dark mahogany in the parlour. Down there all the wood was varnished, heavy serge draped the windows, and from the walls stared grim oil portraits of ancestors, but here in my mother's domain the wood had been painted white, and on pastel walls hung a hundred delicate watercolours: Mum's airy, lovingly detailed renditions of flowers, each picture no larger than a sheet of writing paper, lightly framed.

For a moment I felt as if Mum were here in this room, had been here all the time.

Would that it were so.

Softly, as if I might disturb her, I tiptoed into the next room, her studio: a plain room with bare windows for the sake of light and a bare oak floor for the sake of cleaning. Scanning the easel, the tilted art table, the shelves of paper and supplies, I caught sight of a wooden box and frowned.

Wherever Mum had gone, she had not taken her watercolour kit with her.

But I had assumed—

How very stupid of me. I should have looked here first. She had not gone out to study flowers at all. She had gone—somewhere, some why, I simply did not know, and how had I ever thought I could find her myself? I was stupid, stupid, stupid.

My steps heavy now, I walked through the next door, into Mum's bedroom.

And halted, astonished, for several reasons. First and foremost the state of Mum's shining, modern brass bed: unmade. Every morning of my life, Mum had seen to it that I made my bed and tidied my room immediately after breakfast; surely she would not leave her own bed with linens thrown back and pillows askew and eiderdown comforter sliding onto the Persian carpet?

Moreover, her clothes had not been properly put away. Her brown tweed walking suit had been most carelessly thrown over the top of the standing mirror.

But if not her customary walking outfit—with its

skirt that could be drawn up by strings so that only petticoats need get wet or soiled, yet let down at a moment's notice should a male appear on the horizon—if not this very practical, up-to-date garment for the country, then what had she worn?

Parting the velvet drapes to admit light from the windows, I threw open the wardrobe doors, then stood trying to make sense of the jumble of clothing inside: wool, worsted, muslin, and cotton but also damask, silk, tulle, and velvet. Mum was, you see, very much a free thinker, a woman of character, a proponent of female suffrage and dress reform, including the soft, loose, Aesthetic gowns advocated by Ruskin—but also, whether she liked it or not, she was a squire's widow, with certain obligations. So there were walking costumes and "rationals" but also formal visiting dresses, a low-necked dinner dress, an opera cloak, and a ball gown—the same rusty-purple one Mum had worn for years; she did not care whether she was in fashion. Nor did she throw anything away. There were the black "widow's weeds" she had worn for a year after my father's demise. There was a bronze-green habit left over from her fox-hunting days. There was her grey caped pavement-sweeping suit for city wear. There were fur mantles, quilted satin jackets, paisley skirts, blouses upon blouses . . . I could not make out what garments might be missing from that bewilderment of mauve, maroon, grey-blue, lavender, olive, black, amber, and brown.

Closing the wardrobe doors, I stood puzzled, looking about me.

The entire room was in disarray. The two halves, or "stays," of a corset, along with other unmentionables, lay in plain sight on the marble-topped washstand, and upon the dresser sat a peculiar object like a cushion, but all of a pouf, made of coils and clouds of white horsehair. I lifted this odd thing, rather springy to the touch, and making no sense of it, I carried it along with me on my way out of my mother's rooms.

In the downstairs hallway I encountered Lane polishing the woodwork. Showing him my find, I asked him, "Lane, what is this?"

As a butler, he did his very best to remain expressionless, but he stammered slightly as he replied, "That is, um, ah, a dress improver, Miss Enola."

Dress improver?

But not for the front, surely. Therefore, it must be for the rear.

Oh.

I held in my hands, in a public room of the hall, in the presence of a male, the unwhisperable that hid inside a gentlewoman's bustle, supporting its folds and draperies.

"I beg your pardon!" I exclaimed, feeling the heat of a blush rise in my face. "I had no idea." Never having worn a bustle, I had not seen such an item before. "A thousand apologies." But an urgent thought conquered my embarrassment. "Lane," I asked, "in what manner was my mother dressed when she left the house yesterday morning?"

"It's difficult to recall, miss."

"Was she carrying any sort of baggage or parcel?"

"No, indeed, miss."

"Not even a reticule or hand-bag?"

"No, miss." Mother seldom carried anything of the sort. "I think I would have noticed if she were."

"Was she by chance wearing a costume with a, um . . ." The word *bustle* would be indelicate when speaking to a male. "With a train? With tournure?"

Very unlike her, if so.

But with memory dawning in his eyes, Lane nodded. "I cannot bring to mind her exact apparel,

Miss Enola, but I do recall she wore her Turkey-back jacket."

The kind of jacket that would accommodate a bustle.

"And her high-crowned grey hat."

I knew that hat. Meant to be military in appearance, resembling an upside-down flowerpot, it was sometimes, by the vulgar, called three-storeys-and-a-basement.

"And she carried her walking umbrella."

A long black implement meant to be used like a cane, as sturdy as a gentleman's stick.

How odd that my mother should go out with a mannish umbrella, a mannish hat, yet swishing that most flirtatious feminine tail, a bustle.

CHAPTER THE THIRD

JUST BEFORE DINNERTIME, A BOY BROUGHT
a reply from my brothers:

> ARRIVING FIRST MORNING TRAIN CHAUCERLEA STOP
> PLEASE MEET AT STATION STOP M & S HOLMES

Chaucerlea, the nearest town with a railway station, lay ten miles beyond Kineford.

In order to meet the early train, I would have to set off at dawn.

In preparation, that evening I bathed—quite a bother, dragging the metal tub out from under the bed and placing it before the hearth, hauling buckets of water upstairs and then teakettles of boiling water to pour in for warmth. Mrs. Lane was of no help, for—even though it was summertime—she needs must build a fire in my bedchamber, all the while declaring to the kindling, the coals, and finally the flames that no sane person would bathe on such a damp day. I wanted to wash my hair, also, but I could not do so without Mrs. Lane's assistance, and she developed a sudden rheumatism in her arms while declaring to the towels she was heating, "It's no more than three weeks since the last time, and the weather not nearly warm enough."

I bundled into bed directly after my bath, and Mrs. Lane, still muttering, placed hot water bottles at my feet.

In the morning I brushed my hair a full one hundred strokes, trying to render it glossy, then tied it back with a white ribbon to match my frock—girls of the upper classes *must* wear white, you know, to show every fleck of dirt. I wore my newest, least soiled frock, with very nice white lace pantalets below, and the traditional black stockings with black boots, freshly polished by Lane.

After so much dressing at such an early hour I had no time for breakfast. Snatching a shawl from the rack in the hallway—for it was a very chilly morning — I set off on the bicycle, pedalling hard in order to be on time.

Cycling, I have found, allows one to think without fear of one's facial expressions being observed.

It was a relief, yet hardly a comfort, to think about recent events as I sped through Kineford and turned onto the Chaucerlea Way.

I wondered what in the world had happened to my mother.

Trying not to dwell on that, I wondered whether I would have difficulty finding the railway station, and my brothers.

I wondered why on earth Mum had named my brothers "Mycroft" and "Sherlock." Backwards, their names spelled *Tforcym* and *Kcolrehs*.

I wondered whether Mum was all right.

Think instead about Mycroft and Sherlock.

I wondered whether I would recognise them at the train station. I had not seen them since I was four years old, at Father's funeral; all I remembered of them was that they had seemed very tall in their top-hats draped in black crepe, and severe in their black frock coats, their black gloves, their black armbands, their gleaming black patent leather boots.

I wondered whether Father had really expired of mortification due to my existence, as the village children liked to tell me, or whether he had succumbed to fever and pleurisy as Mum said.

I wondered whether my brothers would recognise me after ten years.

Why they had not visited Mother and me, and why we had not visited them, of course I knew: because of the disgrace I had brought upon my family by being born. My brothers could ill afford to associate with us. Mycroft was a busy, influential man with a career in government service in London, and my brother Sherlock was a famous detective with a book written about him, *A Study in Scarlet,* by his friend and fellow lodger, Dr. John Watson. Mum had bought a copy—

Don't think about Mum.

—and we had both read it. Ever since, I had been dreaming of London, the great seaport, the seat of monarchy, the hub of high society, yet, according to Dr. Watson, "that great cesspool into which all the loungers and idlers of the Empire are irresistibly drained." London, where men in white ties and women decked with diamonds attended the opera while, in the streets, heartless cabbies drove horses to exhaustion, according to another favourite book of mine, *Black Beauty*. London, where scholars read in the British Museum and crowds thronged theatres to be Mesmerised. London, where famous people held séances to communicate with the spirits of the dead, while other famous people tried to scientifically explain how a Spiritualist had levitated himself out of a window and into a waiting carriage.

London, where penniless boys wore rags and ran wild in the streets, never going to school. London, where villains killed ladies of the night—I had no clear idea what these were—and took their babies in order to sell them into slavery. In London there were royalty and cutthroats. In London there were master musicians, master artists, and master criminals who kidnapped children and forced them to labour in dens of iniquity. I had no clear idea what those were, either. But I knew that my brother Sherlock, sometimes employed by royalty, ventured into the dens of iniquity to match wits against thugs, thieves, and the princes of crime. My brother Sherlock was a hero.

I remembered Dr. Watson's listing of my

brother's accomplishments: scholar, chemist, superb violinist, expert marksman, swordsman, singlestick fighter, pugilist, and brilliant deductive thinker.

Then I formed a mental list of my own accomplishments: able to read, write, and do sums; find birds' nests; dig worms and catch fish; and, oh yes, ride a bicycle.

The comparison being so dismal, I stopped thinking to devote my attention to the road, as I had reached the edge of Chaucerlea.

The crowd in the cobbled streets daunted me somewhat. I had to wind my way among persons and vehicles unknown in the dirt lanes of Kineford: men selling fruit from barrows, women with baskets peddling sweets, nannies pushing prams, too many pedestrians trying not to be run over by too many carts, coaches, and gigs, beer-wagons and coal-wagons and lumber-wagons, a carriage, even an omnibus pulled by no less than four horses. Amid all this, how was I to find the railway station?

Wait. I saw something. Rising over the house-tops like an ostrich feather upon a lady's hat stood a white plume in the grey sky. The smoke of a steam locomotive.

Pedalling towards it, I soon heard a roaring,

shrieking, clanging noise—the engine coming in. I arrived at the platform just as it did.

Only a few passengers got off, and among them I had no difficulty recognising two tall male Londoners who had to be my brothers. They wore gentlemen's country attire: dark tweed suits with braid edging, soft ties, bowler hats. And kid gloves. Only gentry wore gloves at the height of summer. One of my brothers had grown a bit stout, showing an expanse of silk waistcoat. That would be Mycroft, I supposed, the older by seven years. The other—Sherlock—stood straight as a rake and lean as a greyhound in his charcoal suit and black boots.

Swinging their walking sticks, they turned their heads from side to side, looking for something, but their scrutiny passed right over me.

Meanwhile, everyone on the platform stole glances at them.

And to my annoyance, I found myself trembling as I hopped off my bicycle. A strip of lace from my pantalets, confounded flimsy things, caught on the chain, tore loose, and dangled over my left boot.

Trying to tuck it up, I dropped my shawl.

This would not do. Taking a deep breath, leaving my shawl on my bicycle and my bicycle leaning against the station wall, I straightened and approached the two Londoners, not quite succeeding in holding my head high.

"Mr. Holmes," I asked, "and, um, Mr. Holmes?"

Two pairs of sharp grey eyes fixed upon me. Two pairs of aristocratic brows lifted.

I said, "You, um, you asked me to meet you here."

"Enola?" they both exclaimed at once, and then in rapid alternation:

"What are you doing here? Why did you not send the carriage?"

"We should have known her; she looks just like you, Sherlock." The taller, leaner one was indeed Sherlock, then. I liked his bony face, his hawk eyes, his nose like a beak, but I sensed that for me to look like him was no compliment.

"I thought she was a street urchin."

"On a bicycle?"

"Why the bicycle? Where's the carriage, Enola?"

I blinked: Carriage? There were a landau and a phaeton gathering dust in the carriage house, but there had been no horses for many years, not since my mother's old hunter had gone on to greener pastures.

"I could have hired horses, I suppose," I said

slowly, "but I would not know how to harness or drive them."

The stout one, Mycroft, exclaimed, "Why are we paying a stable boy, then, and a groom?"

"I beg your pardon?"

"Are you telling me there are no horses?"

"Later, Mycroft. You!" With commanding ease, Sherlock summoned a loitering lad. "Go hire us a brougham." He tossed a coin to the boy, who touched his cap and ran off.

"We had better wait inside," Mycroft said. "Out here in the wind, Enola's hair more and more resembles a jackdaw's nest. Where's your hat, Enola?"

By then, somehow, the moment had passed for me to say, "How do you do" or for them to say, "So nice to see you again, my dear" and shake hands, or something of that sort, even though I was the shame of the family. By then, also, I was beginning to realise that PLEASE MEET AT STATION had been a request for transportation, not for me to present myself in person.

Well, if they did not desire the pleasure of my conversation, it was a good thing, as I stood mute and stupid.

"Or your gloves," Sherlock chided, taking me by

the arm and steering me towards the station, "or decent, decorous clothing of any sort? You're a young lady now, Enola."

That statement alarmed me into speech. "I've only just turned fourteen."

In puzzled, almost plaintive tones Mycroft murmured, "But I've been paying for the seamstress . . ."

Speaking to me, Sherlock decreed in that offhand imperial way of his, "You should have been in long skirts since you were twelve. What ever was your mother thinking of? I suppose she's gone over entirely to the Suffragists?"

"I don't know where she's gone," I said, and to my own surprise — for I had not wept until that moment — I burst into tears.

Further mention of Mum, then, was put off until we sat in the hired brougham, with my bicycle strapped on behind, swaying along towards Kineford. "We are a pair of thoughtless brutes," Sherlock had observed to Mycroft at one point, while providing me with a large, very starchy handkerchief hardly comforting to the nose. I am sure they thought I was weeping for my mum — as I was. But truthfully, I wept also for myself.

Enola.

Alone.

Shoulder to shoulder on the seat opposite me, my brothers sat together, facing me yet looking at anything else. Plainly they found me an embarrassment.

I quieted my sniffling within a few minutes of leaving the railway station, but I could not think of anything to say. A brougham, being little more than a wheeled box with small windows, does not encourage conversation, even if I were inclined to point out the beauties of nature, which I most definitely was not.

"So, Enola," asked Mycroft gruffly after a while, "are you feeling well enough to tell us what has happened?"

I did so, but there was little to add to what they already knew. Mum had left home early on Tuesday morning and had not returned since. No, she had left me no message or explanation of any sort. No, there was no reason to think she might have taken ill; her health was excellent. No, there had been no word of her from anyone. No, in answer to Sherlock's questions, there had been no bloodstains, no footprints, no signs of forced entry, and I did not know of any strangers who had been lurking about.

No, there had been no ransom demand. If Mum had any enemies, I did not know of them. Yes, I had notified the Kineford police constabulary.

"So I can see," Sherlock remarked, leaning forward to peer out the window of the brougham as we rolled into Ferndell Park, "for there they are, along with every loiterer in the village, prodding the bushes and peering about in the most ineffectual manner."

"Do they expect to find her sheltering under a hawthorn?" Grunting as his frontal amplitude got in his way, Mycroft leaned forward to look in his turn. His bushy eyebrows shot up under the brim of his hat. "What," he cried, "has been done to the grounds?"

Startled, I protested, "Nothing!"

"Absolutely, nothing has been done, apparently for years! All is sorely overgrown—"

"Interesting," Sherlock murmured.

"Barbaric!" Mycroft retorted. "Grass a foot tall, saplings springing up, gorse, bramble bushes—"

"Those are wild roses." I liked them.

"Growing on what should be the front lawn? How, pray tell, does the gardener earn his pay?"

"Gardener? There is no gardener."

Mycroft turned on me like a hawk stooping. "But you do have a gardener! Ruggles, the man's name is, and I have been paying him twelve shillings a week for the past ten years!"

I daresay I sat with my mouth open, for several reasons. How could Mycroft be suffering under this absurd delusion that there was a gardener? I knew no one named Ruggles. Moreover, I had no idea that money came from Mycroft. I think I'd been assuming that money, like stair rails and chandeliers and other furnishings, came with the hall.

Sherlock intervened. "Mycroft, if there were such a personage, I am sure Enola would be well aware of him."

"Bah. She wasn't aware of—"

Sherlock interrupted, although addressing his remark to me. "Enola, never mind. Mycroft gets quite out of humour when he is disrupted from his usual orbit between his rooms, his office, and the Diogenes Club."

Ignoring him, his brother leaned towards me, demanding, "Enola, are there really no horses, no groom, and no stable boy?"

"No. I mean, yes." Yes, there really were none.

"Well, which is it, no or yes?"

"Mycroft," Sherlock intervened, "the girl's head, you'll observe, is rather small in proportion to her remarkably tall body. Let her alone. There is no use in confusing and upsetting her when you'll find out for yourself soon enough."

Indeed, at that moment the hired brougham pulled up in front of Ferndell Hall.

CHAPTER THE FOURTH

ENTERING MY MOTHER'S ROOMS ALONG with my brothers, I noticed upon the tea table a Japanese vase with flowers in it, their petals going brown. Mum must have arranged that bouquet a day or two before she had gone missing.

I picked up the vase and hugged it to my chest.

Sherlock Holmes swept past me. He had rebuffed Lane's welcome, declined Mrs. Lane's offer of a cup of tea, refused to pause even a moment before beginning his investigation. Glancing about my mother's light, airy sitting room with its many watercolours of flowers, he then strode through the studio and onward into the bedchamber. There I heard him give a sharp exclamation.

"What is it?" called Mycroft, ambling in more

slowly, having chatted a moment with Lane as he left his stick, hat, and gloves in the butler's care.

"Deplorable!" cried Sherlock from the far room, referring, I assumed, to the mess in general and the unmentionables in particular. "Indecent!" Yes, definitely the unmentionables. Striding out of the bedroom, he reappeared in the studio. "She seems to have left in great haste."

Seems, I thought.

"Or perhaps she has become lax in her personal habits," he added more calmly. "She is, after all, sixty-four years old."

The vase of flowers in my arms gave off an odour of stagnant water and decaying stems. When it was fresh, however, the bouquet must have smelled wonderful. The shrivelled blossoms, I saw, had been sweet peas.

And thistles.

"Sweet peas and thistles?" I exclaimed. "How odd."

Both men turned their eyes upon me with some exasperation. "Your mother *was* odd," said Sherlock curtly.

"And still is, presumably," added Mycroft more

gently, for my benefit, judging by the warning glance he gave his brother.

So they, too, feared she might be . . . deceased.

In the same sharp tone Sherlock said, "From the state of affairs here, it appears she may now have progressed from oddness to senile dementia."

Hero or no hero, he—his manner—was beginning to annoy me. And distress me, for my mother was his mother, too; how could he be so cold?

I did not know then, had no way of knowing, that Sherlock Holmes lived his life in a kind of chill shadow. He suffered from melancholia, the fits sometimes coming upon him so badly that for a week or more he would refuse to rise from his bed.

"Senility?" Mycroft asked. "Can you not arrive at any more helpful deduction?"

"Such as?"

"You're the detective. Whip out that lens of yours. *Detect.*"

"I have already done so. There is nothing to be learned here."

"Outside, then?"

"After a full day of rain? There will be no traces to tell which way she's gone. Foolish woman."

Dismayed by his tone and this comment, I left, carrying the vase of withering flowers downstairs to the kitchen.

There I found Mrs. Lane crouched upon the floor with a scrub brush, scouring the oak boards so fiercely that I suspected she, also, was perturbed in her mind.

I dumped the contents of the Japanese vase into the wooden slop bucket, on top of vegetable parings and such.

On her hands and knees, Mrs. Lane told the floor, "Here I was so looking forward to seeing Mister Mycroft and Mister Sherlock again."

Setting the green-slimed vase in the lead-lined wooden sink, I ran water into it from the cistern tap.

Mrs. Lane spoke on, "And here it's still the same old story, the same foolish quarrel, they've never a kind word for their own mother, and she maybe lying out there . . ."

Her voice actually broke. I said nothing, so as not to further upset her.

Sniffing and scrubbing, Mrs. Lane declared, "Small wonder they're bachelors. Must have everything their way. Think it's their right. Never could abide a strong-minded woman."

A bell rang, one of a number of bells poised on coiled wires along the wall above the stove.

"There, now, that's the morning room bell. I suppose that's them wanting luncheon, and me up to my elbows in the dirt of this floor."

Having had no breakfast, I quite wanted luncheon myself. Also, I wanted to know what was going on. I left the kitchen and went to the morning room.

At that informal room's small table sat Sherlock smoking a pipe and staring at Mycroft, who sat across from him.

"The two best thinkers in England ought to be able to reason this out," Mycroft was saying. "Now, has Mother gone off voluntarily, or was she planning to return? The untidy state of her room—"

"Could mean that she left impulsively and in haste, or it could reflect the innate untidiness of a woman's mind," interrupted Sherlock. "Of what use is reason when it comes to the dealings of a woman, and very likely one in her dotage?"

Both of them glanced up at me as I entered the room, appearing hopeful that I might be a housemaid, although they should have known by now that there were none. "Luncheon?" Mycroft asked.

"Heaven knows," I replied as I sat down at the table with them. "Mrs. Lane is in an uncertain frame of mind."

"Indeed."

I studied my tall, handsome (to me at least), brilliant brothers. I admired them. I wanted to like them. I wanted *them* to—

Nonsense, Enola. You'll do very well on your own.

As for my brothers, they paid me no further heed.

"I assure you, Mother is neither in her dotage, nor demented," said Mycroft to Sherlock. "No senile woman could have compiled the accounts she has sent me over the past ten years, perfectly clear and orderly, detailing the expense of installing a bathroom—"

"Which does not exist," interrupted Sherlock in acid tones.

"—and water closet—"

"Likewise."

"—and the constantly rising salaries of the footmen, the housemaids, the kitchen maid, and the daily help—"

"Nonexistent."

"—the gardener, the under-gardener, the odd man—"

"Also nonexistent, unless one considers Dick."

"Who is quite odd," Mycroft agreed. A joke, yet I saw no flicker of a smile on either of my brothers. "I'm surprised Mother did not list one Reginald Collie, who is arguably a servant, in her expenses. She listed imaginary horses and ponies, imaginary carriages, a coachman, grooms, stable boys—"

"There is no denying that we have been woefully deceived."

"—and for Enola, a music teacher, a dancing instructor, a governess—"

A startled look passed between them, as if a logic problem had suddenly grown a face and hair, and then both at once they turned to stare at me.

"Enola," Sherlock demanded, "you *have* at least had a governess, haven't you?"

I had not. Mum had sent me to school with the village children, and after I had learned all I could there, she had told me I would do quite well on my own, and I considered that I had. I'd read every book in Ferndell Hall's library, from *A Child's Garden of Verses* to the entire *Encyclopaedia Britannica*.

As I hesitated, Mycroft restated the question: "You have had the proper education of a young lady?"

"I have read Shakespeare," I replied, "and Aristotle, and Locke, and the novels of Thackeray, and the essays of Mary Wollstonecraft."

Their faces froze. I could scarcely have horrified them more if I had told them I had learned to perform on a circus trapeze.

Then Sherlock turned to Mycroft and said softly, "It's my fault. There's no trusting a woman; why make an exception for one's mother? I should have come here to check upon her yearly at the very least, no matter how much unpleasantness would have ensued."

Mycroft said just as softly and sadly, "To the contrary, my dear Sherlock, it is I who have neglected my responsibility. I am the elder son —"

A discreet cough sounded, and in came Lane with a tray of cucumber sandwiches, sliced fruit, and a pitcher of lemonade. There was blessed silence for a few moments until luncheon was served.

During that silence, I framed a question. "What has any of this," I asked after Lane had withdrawn, "to do with finding Mother?"

Rather than answering me, Mycroft gave his full attention to his plate.

Sherlock drummed his fingers, rumpling the starched lace tablecloth. "We are formulating a theory," he said at last.

"And what is this theory?"

Silence again.

I asked, "Am I to have my mother back again or not?"

Neither of them would look at me, but after what seemed a long time, Sherlock glanced at his brother and said, "Mycroft, I think she has a right to know."

Mycroft sighed, nodded, put down what remained of his third sandwich, and faced me. "We are trying to decide," he said, "whether what is happening now connects to what happened after Father's dea— er, after our father's passing away. You wouldn't remember, I suppose."

"I was four years old," I said. "I remember mostly the black horses."

"Quite so. Well, after the burial, over the next few days there was disagreement—"

"That's putting it kindly," Sherlock interposed. "The words 'battle royal' come to mind."

Ignoring him, Mycroft went on. "Disagreement

as to the handling of the estate. Neither Sherlock nor I wanted to live here, so Mother thought that the rent money should come directly to her, and that she should run Ferndell Park."

Well, she did run it, didn't she? Yet Mycroft sounded as if he considered the idea absurd.

"As I am the firstborn son, the estate is mine," he went on, "and Mother did not dispute that, but she could not seem to see why she should not manage things for me, rather than the other way around. When Sherlock and I reminded her that, legally, she had no right even to live here unless I permitted it, she became quite irrational and made it clear that we were no longer welcome in our own birthplace."

Oh. My goodness. Everything seemed to turn upside down in my mind, as if it were swinging by its knees from a tree limb. All my life I had assumed that my brothers kept their distance due to my shameful existence, whereas they were saying—a quarrel with my mother?

I could not tell how Mycroft felt regarding this revelation. Or Sherlock.

I could not quite tell how I felt about it, either,

other than bewildered. But something secret fluttered like a butterfly in my heart.

"I sent her a monthly allowance," Mycroft went on, "and she wrote me a very businesslike letter requesting an increase. I replied by asking for an accounting of how the money was being spent, and she complied. Her continuing requests for additional funds seemed so reasonable that I never refused any of them. But, as we now know, her accounts were fictitious. What actually has become of all that money, we, um, we have no idea."

I noticed his hesitation. "But you have a theory," I said.

"Yes." He took a long breath. "We think she has been hoarding, while planning an escapade, all this time." Another breath, even longer. "We think she has now taken what she perceives as her money and, um, gone somewhere to, ah, thumb her nose at us, so to speak."

What on earth was he saying? That Mum had abandoned me? I sat with my mouth ajar.

"Pity the girl's cranial capacity, Mycroft," Sherlock murmured to his brother, and to me he said gently, "Enola, simply put, we think she has run away."

But—but that was preposterous, impossible. She wouldn't have done that to me.

"No," I blurted. "No, it can't be."

"Think, Enola." Sherlock sounded just like Mum. "All logic points to that conclusion. If she were injured, the searchers would have found her, and if she were in an accident, we would have heard. There is no reason for anyone to harm her, and there are no signs of foul play. There is no reason for anyone to seize her against her will, other than ransom, for which there has been no demand." He paused for a significant breath before going on. "If, however, she is alive, in good health, and doing whatever she pleases—"

"As usual," Mycroft put in.

"Her disorderly bedroom could be the merest blind."

"To throw us off the track," Mycroft agreed. "It certainly appears that she has been plotting and scheming for years—"

I sat up straight like a steam whistle. "But if she could have left anytime," I wailed, "why would she do it on my *birthday*?"

Now it was their turn to sit with mouths slack and uncouth. I had bested them.

But at that very triumphant instant it occurred to me, with a chill, that Mum *had* instructed Mrs. Lane to give me my gifts, just in case she were not back in time for tea.

Or for ever.

CHAPTER THE FIFTH

BECAUSE MY EYES BURNED WITH TEARS, I am afraid I excused myself from luncheon rather hastily.

I needed to be outside. Fresh air would cool my heated feelings. Pausing only to snatch up the new drawing kit Mum had given me, I ran out the kitchen door, through the vegetable garden, past the empty stables, across the overgrown lawn, and into the wooded portion of the estate. Then, out of breath, I walked on beneath the oaks, feeling somewhat better.

It seemed I was alone in the forest. The constables and other searchers had passed on to the more distant fields and moorlands.

The woodland sloped downward, and at the bottom of that incline I reached my favourite place, the deep rocky dell where ferns draped like a lady's green velvet evening gown over the stones, trailing down to a pebbly stream that formed a pool under a leaning willow. Heedless of my frock and pantalets, I clambered over rocks and ferns until I reached the willow. Hugging its stout trunk, I laid my cheek against its mossy bark. Then I ducked beneath it to crawl into a shady hollow between the overhanging tree and the stream.

This cool nook was my secret hideaway, known to no one except me. Here I kept things I liked, things Mrs. Lane would have thrown out if I had brought them into the house. As my eyes grew accustomed to the shadows, I settled into my earthy den, looking around me at little shelves I had built of stones. Yes, there were my snail shells, my many-coloured pebbles, my acorn caps, some bright jay feathers, a cuff-link and a broken locket and other such treasures I had found in magpies' nests.

With a sigh of relief I curled my knees up to my chin in a most unladylike fashion, wrapped my arms around my shins, and gazed at the eddying water just beyond my feet. Trout fingerlings swam in the pool. Watching them dart and school, dart and school, usually I could Mesmerise myself into a sort of daze.

But not today. All I could think was what could have become of Mum, how I would have to go home eventually and she would not be awaiting me, but my brothers would, and when I entered with a great deal of dirt all over my frock, they would say—

A pox on my brothers.

Putting my knees down where they belonged, I opened my new drawing kit to take pencil in hand, and a few sheets of paper. On one of these I drew a hasty, not particularly nice picture of Mycroft in his spats and his monocle and his heavy pocket-watch chain looped across his protruding waistcoat.

Then I drew a similarly quick picture of Sherlock, all lanky legs and nose and chin.

Then I wanted to draw Mum, for I was angry at her, too. I wanted to sketch her as she might have looked the day she went away, in her hat like an upside-down flowerpot, Turkey-back jacket, and a bustle, so ridiculous . . .

And she hadn't taken her art kit with her.

And she hadn't expected to be back for my birthday celebration.

She *had* been up to something. Much as it hurt, I admitted it now.

Confound her, the whole time I'd been searching for her in a panic, she had been doing very well on her own, enjoying some adventure without me.

One would think I might feel glad to conclude that she was alive.

Quite to the contrary. I felt wretched.

She had abandoned me.

Why hadn't she just cast me off in the first place? Put me in a basket and left me on a doorstep when I was born?

Why had she left me now?

Where might she have gone?

Instead of sketching, I sat thinking. Laying aside my drawings, I wrote a list of questions:

Why did Mum not take me with her?

If she had any distance to travel, why did she not use the bicycle?

Why did she dress so oddly?

Why did she not leave by the gate?

If she struck out across country, on foot, where was she going?

Supposing she found transportation, again,
  where was she going?
What did she do with all the money?
If she were running away, why did she
  carry no baggage?
Why would she run away on my birthday?
Why did she leave me no word of explanation or farewell?

Putting down my pencil, I stared at the eddying stream, the fingerlings flowing past like dark tears.

Something rustled in the underbrush that flanked the willow. As I turned to look, a familiar furry head poked into my hollow.

"Oh, Reginald," I complained, "let me alone." But I leaned towards the old collie. He thrust his broad, blunt snout at my face, fanning his tail as I put my arms around his shaggy neck.

"Thank you, Reginald," said a cultured voice. My brother Sherlock stood over me.

Gasping, I pushed Reginald away and reached for the papers I had left lying on the ground. But not quickly enough. Sherlock picked them up first.

He gawked at my drawings of Mycroft and himself, then threw his head back and laughed almost silently yet quite heartily, rocking back and forth until he had to sit down on a shelf of rock beside the willow tree, gasping for breath.

I felt on fire with mortification, but he was smiling. "Well done, Enola," he chuckled when he could speak. "You have quite the knack for caricature." He gave the sketches back to me. "It would perhaps be best if Mycroft were not to see those."

Keeping my red face down, I slipped the papers into the bottom of the drawing kit.

My brother said, "Sometime that tree is going to tumble right into the water, you know, and it is to be hoped you will not be underneath it when that happens."

He was not mocking my hideaway, at least, but I felt a mild reproach in his words, and his desire for me to come out. Frowning, I did so.

He asked, "What is that paper you have in your hand? May I see?"

My list. I gave it to him, telling myself I didn't care anymore what he thought of me.

I sat, slumping, on another fern-upholstered rock as he read.

He paid close attention to my list. Indeed, he pondered it, his narrow, hawk-nosed face quite serious now.

"You have certainly covered the salient points," he said finally, with some small air of surprise. "I think we can surmise that she did not leave by the gate because she did not want the lodge-keeper to see in which direction she was going. And for the same reason she did not want to use the roads, where she might meet with some witness. She has been clever enough to leave us with no idea whether she went north, south, east, or west."

I nodded, sitting up straighter, feeling unaccountably better. My brother Sherlock had not laughed at my thoughts. He was talking with me.

That nameless butterfly fluttering in my heart— I began to sense now what it was.

It had started when I had found out that my brothers' quarrel was with my mother, not with me.

It was—a hope. A dream. A yearning, really. Now that there might be a chance.

I wanted my brothers to . . . I did not dare to think in terms of affection, but I wanted them to care for me a little, somehow.

Sherlock was saying, "As for your other points, Enola, I hope to clear them up very soon."

I nodded again.

"One question I do not understand. While I asked Lane for a description of your mother's attire, I fail to see how it was odd."

I blushed, remembering my shocking blunder with Lane, and only just managed to murmur, "The, um, tournure."

"Ah. The bustle." It was perfectly all right for him to say it. "As the cannibal asked the missionary's wife, are all your women so deformed? Well, there is no accounting for the ways ladies choose to adorn themselves. The whims of the fair sex defy logic." He shrugged, dismissing the subject. "Enola, I am returning to London within the hour; therefore I searched you out in order to say good-bye to you and tell you it has been delightful to see you again after all these years."

He offered his hand—gloved, of course. I grasped it for a moment. I could not speak.

"Mycroft will remain here for a few days," Sherlock went on, "little as he cares to be away from his dear Diogenes Club."

After swallowing to regain my voice, I asked, "What will you do in London?"

"File an inquiry with Scotland Yard. Search the passenger lists of steamship companies for women travelling alone, in case, as we hypothesise, our straying mother has left England for the south of France or some such artistic mecca . . . or perhaps she is making a pilgrimage to some shrine of the Suffragists." He looked at me quite levelly. "Enola, you have known her more recently than I. Where do *you* think she might have gone?"

The great Sherlock Holmes asking me for my thoughts? But I had none to offer. I was, after all, a girl of minimal cranial capacity. Feeling the heat of a blush once more start to burn its way up my neck, I shook my head.

"Well, the constabulary reports not a sign of her hereabouts, so I am off." He stood up, touching the brim of his hat as a courtesy, not quite tipping it to me. "Take heart," he told me. "There is no indication that she has come to any harm." Then, swinging his stick, he walked up the rocks of the dell with easy dignity, as if ascending a marble stairway to some London palace. Reaching the top, without turning he raised his cane, waggling it in a kind of dismissal or farewell, then strode off towards the hall with the dog trotting adoringly after him.

I watched him until he disappeared between the forest trees—watched after him almost as if I knew that, through no fault of his own, I would not converse with him again for a long time.

Back at the hall, I went looking for the item Lane had called a "dress improver," finding it where I had left it, most inappropriately, in the front parlour. I wondered why Mum had put the featherweight cushion upon her dresser, yet had not worn it inside her bustle. Pondering, I took it and walked upstairs to replace it in her bedroom in case she wanted it when she—

Returned?

But there was no reason to think she would ever return.

She had, after all, chosen to leave. Of her own free will.

Sinking into the hard wooden arms of a hallway

chair, I slumped like a comma over the prickly pouf of horsehair I held. I stayed that way for a long time.

Finally I lifted my head, vengeful thoughts hardening my jaw. If Mum had left me behind, I was very well going to help myself to the contents of her rooms.

This was a decision prompted partly by spleen, partly by necessity. Having ruined my frock, I needed to change it. The few others I owned, formerly white, now yellow-green with dirt and grass stains, only looked worse. I would choose something out of Mum's wardrobe.

Rising, I strode across the upstairs hallway to my mother's door and turned the knob.

To no good effect. The door was locked.

It had been a most annoying day. Stalking to the stairs, leaning over the banister, I allowed my voice to rise to a naughty pitch. "Lane!"

"Shhh!" Amazingly—for he could have been anywhere from the chimney to the cellar—the butler appeared below me within a moment. One white-gloved finger to his lips, he informed me, "Miss Enola, Mr. Mycroft is napping."

Rolling my eyes, I beckoned Lane to come upstairs. When he had done so, I told him more quietly, "I need the key to Mother's rooms."

"Mr. Mycroft has given orders that those rooms are to be kept locked."

Astonishment trumped my annoyance. "What ever for?"

"It's not my place to ask, Miss Enola."

"Very well. I don't need the key if you'll just un-lock the door for me."

"I should have to ask Mr. Mycroft's permission, Miss Enola, and if I awaken him, he will be put out. Mr. Mycroft has given orders—"

Mr. Mycroft this, Mr. Mycroft that, Mr. Mycroft could go soak his head in a rain-barrel. Tight-lipped, I thrust the dress improver at Lane. "I need to put this back where it belongs."

The butler actually blushed, which gratified me, as I had not seen him do so ever before.

"Moreover," I continued quite softly between my clenched teeth, "I need to search my mother's wardrobe for something to wear. If I go down to dinner in this frock, Mr. Mycroft will be more than put out. He will froth at the mouth. Unlock the door."

Without another word, Lane did so. But he himself kept the key and stood outside the door, waiting for me.

Therefore, filled with the spirit of perversity, I took my time. But as I scanned my mother's dresses, I thought also about this new development. Locked door to Mum's rooms, entry with Mycroft's permission only—this would never do.

I wondered whether Mum might possibly have left her own key behind.

The thought frightened me, for if—dressing to go out for the day—if she had intended to return, she would have taken the key with her.

Therefore, if she had left it behind—the meaning was all too plain.

It took me a moment and several deep breaths to make myself reach for her walking suit, which still hung over the standing mirror.

I found the key at once, in a jacket pocket.

It felt heavy in my hand. I stood looking at it as if I had never seen it before. Oval handle on one end of the shank, toothed rectangle on the other. Strange, cold iron thing.

She really wasn't planning to come back, then.

Yet this hateful skeleton of metal had suddenly become my most precious possession. Clutching it,

I draped a dress from my mother's wardrobe over my hand to conceal it, and went out again.

"Very well, Lane," I told him blandly, and he once more locked the door.

At dinner, Mycroft had the courtesy to say not a word about my borrowed dress, a loose, flowing Aesthetic gown, which bared my neck but hung upon the rest of me like a sheet upon a broomstick. Although I was as tall as Mum, I lacked her womanly figure, and in any event, I had chosen the dress for its colour—peach touched with cream, which I loved—not for any pretense of fit. It dragged on the floor, but very well, thus it concealed my little-girl boots. I had tied a sash around my straight-as-a-poker middle to resemble a waist; I wore a necklace; I had even tried to arrange my hair, although its indefinite brownish hue made it hardly a crowning beauty. Altogether, I am sure I looked like a child playing dress-up, and I knew it.

Mycroft, although he said nothing, clearly was not pleased. As soon as the fish was served, he told me, "I have sent to London for a seamstress to provide you with proper clothing."

I nodded. Some new clothes would be nice, and

if I didn't like them, I could revert to my comfortable knickerbockers the moment his back was turned. But I said, "There is a seamstress right here in Kineford."

"Yes, I am aware of that. But the London seamstress will know exactly what you need for boarding school."

Whatever was he talking about? Quite patiently I said, "I am not going to boarding school."

Just as patiently he responded, "Of course you are, Enola. I have sent inquiries to several excellent establishments for young ladies."

Mother had told me about such establishments. Her Rational Dress journals were filled with warnings about their cultivation of the "hourglass" figure. At one such "school," the headmistress tightened a corset upon each girl who entered, and on the girl's waist the corset stayed, day and night, waking or sleeping, except for one hour a week when it was removed for "ablutions," that is, so that the girl could bathe. Then it was replaced, tighter, depriving the wearer of the ability to breathe normally, so that the slightest shock would cause her to fall down in a faint. This was considered "charming." It was also considered moral, the corset being "an ever-present monitor bidding its wearer to exercise self-restraint"—in other words, making it impossible for the hapless victim to bend or relax her posture. The modern corsets, unlike my mother's old whalebone ones, were so long that they needed to be made of steel so as not to break, their rigidity displacing the internal organs and deforming the ribcage. One schoolgirl's corseted ribs had actually punctured her lungs, causing her untimely demise. Her waist as she lay in her coffin had measured fifteen inches.

All of this passed through my mind in an instant as my fork dropped to my plate with a clatter. I sat stunned, chilled by the horror of my situation, yet unable to state any of my objections to my brother. To speak of such intimate matters of the female form to a male was unthinkable. I was able only to gasp, "But, Mother—"

"There is no assurance that your mother will come back anytime soon. I cannot stay here indefinitely." Thank goodness, I thought. "And you can't just vegetate here by yourself, now, can you, Enola?"

"Are Lane and Mrs. Lane not to stay on?"

He frowned, putting down the knife with which he had been buttering his bread. "Of course, but servants cannot possibly provide you with proper instruction and supervision."

"I was about to say, Mother would not like—"

"Your mother has failed in her responsibility to you." His tone had grown considerably sharper than the butter knife. "What is to become of you if you do not acquire some accomplishments, some social graces, some finish? You will never be able to move in polite society, and your prospects of matrimony—"

"Are dim to nil in any event," I said, "as I look just like Sherlock."

I think my candor staggered him. "My dear girl." His tone softened. "That will change, or it will be changed." By my sitting for endless hours with a book on top of my head while playing the piano, I supposed. Days spent in torment, plus corsets, dress improvers, and false hair, although he would not say so. "You come from a family of quality, and with some polishing, I am sure you will not disgrace us."

I said, "I have always been a disgrace, I will always be a disgrace, and I am not going to be sent to any finishing establishment for young ladies."

"Yes, you are."

Glaring across the table at each other in the candle-lit twilight, we had given up any pretense of dining. I am sure he was aware, as I was, that both Lane and Mrs. Lane were eavesdropping in the hallway, but I, for one, did not care.

I raised my voice. "No. Get me a governess if you must, but I am not going to any so-called boarding school. You cannot make me go."

He actually softened his tone, but said, "Yes, I can, and I shall."

"What do you mean? Shall you shackle me to take me there?"

He rolled his eyes. "Just like her mother," he declared to the ceiling, and then he fixed upon me a stare so martyred, so condescending, that I froze rigid. In tones of sweetest reason he told me, "Enola, legally I hold complete charge over both your mother and you. I can, if I wish, lock you in your room until you become sensible, or take whatever other measures are necessary in order to achieve that desired result. Moreover, as your older brother I bear a moral responsibility for you, and it is plain to see that you have run wild too long. I am perhaps only just in time to save you from a wasted life. You *will* do as I say."

In that moment I understood exactly how Mum had felt during those days after my father's death.

And why she had made no attempt to visit my brothers in London, or welcomed them to Ferndell Park.

And why she had tricked money out of Mycroft.

I stood up. "Dinner no longer appeals to me. You'll excuse me, I'm sure."

I wish I could say I swept with cold dignity out of the room, but the truth is, I tripped over my skirt and stumbled to the stairs.

CHAPTER THE SIXTH

THAT NIGHT I COULD NOT SLEEP. INDEED, at first I could not even be still. In my nightgown, barefoot, I paced, paced, paced my bedroom as I imagined a lion at the London Zoo might pace his cage. Later, when I turned my coal-oil lamp low, put out my candles, and went to bed, my eyes would not close. I heard Mycroft retire to the guest bedroom; I heard Lane and Mrs. Lane tread upstairs to their quarters on the top floor, and still I lay staring at the shadows.

The whole reason for my distress was not as obvious as may at first appear. It was Mycroft who had made me angry, but it was my changing thoughts about my mother that made me upset, almost queasy. It feels very queer to think of one's mother as a person like oneself, not just a mum, so to speak. Yet there it was: She had been weak as well as strong. She had felt as trapped as I did. She had felt the injustice of her situation just as keenly. She had been forced to obey, as I would be forced to obey. She had wanted to rebel, as I desperately yearned to rebel, without knowing how I ever would or could.

But in the end, she had managed it. Glorious rebellion.

Confound her, why had she not taken me with her?

Kicking off the covers to lunge out of bed, I turned up the oil lamp, stalked to my desk—its border of stencilled flowers did not cheer me now— seized paper and pencil from my drawing kit, and drew a furious picture of my mother, all wrinkles and jowls with her mouth a thin line, going off in her three-storeys-and-a-basement hat and her turkey-back jacket, flourishing her umbrella like a sword while the train of her ridiculous bustle trailed behind her.

Why had she not taken me into her confidence? *Why* had she left me behind?

Oh, very well, I could understand, however painfully, that she had not wanted to trust a young girl with her secret . . . but why had she not at least offered me some message of explanation or farewell?

And why, oh why, had she chosen to leave on my *birthday?* Mum never in her life took a stitch without thread. She must have had a reason. What could it be?

Because . . .

I sat bolt upright at the desk, my mouth agape.

Now I saw.

From Mum's point of view.

And it made perfect sense. Mum was clever. Clever, clever, clever.

She *had* left me a message.

As a present.

On my birthday. Which was why she had chosen that day of all days to leave. A day for the giving of gifts, so no one would notice —

I leapt up. Where had I put it? I had to light a candle to carry with me so I could see to look around my bedroom. It was not on the bookshelf. It was not on any of the chairs, or my dresser, or my wash-stand, or my bed. It was not perched on the Noah's Ark or the rocking horse, hand-me-downs from my brothers. Confound my stupid, muddled head, where had I put . . . there. In my neglected dollhouse, of all places, there it was: a slender sheaf of hand-painted, hand-lettered crisp artists' papers, creased precisely in half and stitched together along the fold.

I pounced upon it: the booklet of ciphers my mother had created for me.

ALO NEK OOL NIY MSM UME HTN
ASY RHC

In my mother's flyaway lettering.

One glance at the first cipher made me shut my eyes, wanting to cry.

Think, Enola.

It was almost as if I heard my mother chiding me from inside my head. "Enola, you'll do quite well on your own."

I opened my eyes, stared at the line of jumbled letters, and thought.

Very well. First of all, a sentence would not likely have words all of three letters.

Taking a fresh sheet of paper from my drawing kit, I pulled close the oil lamp on one hand and the candle on the other, then copied the cipher like this:

ALONEKOOLNIYMSMUMEHTNASYRHC

The first word sprang out at me: "alone."
Or was it "Enola"?
Try it backwards.

CHRYSANTHEMUMSMYINLOOKENOLA

My eye passed over the first part to seize upon the letters "MUM." Mum. Mother was sending me a message about herself?

MUMS MY IN LOOK ENOLA

The order of the words sounded backwards.

ENOLA LOOK IN MY

Oh, for Heaven's sake. CHRYSANTHE-MUMS. The border of flowers painted around the page should have told me. Gold and russet chrysan-themums.

I had solved the cipher.

I was not totally stupid.

Or perhaps I was, for what on earth did it mean, "Enola, look in my chrysanthemums"? Had Mother buried something in a flower bed somewhere? Unlikely. I doubted she'd ever held a shovel in her life. Dick took care of such chores, and in any event, Mother was no gardener; she liked to let hardy flowers, such as the chrysanthemums, take care of themselves.

The chrysanthemums outside. What would she consider *her* chrysanthemums?

Downstairs the casement clock struck two. Never before had I been up so late at night. My mind felt as if it were floating, not quite anchored in my head anymore.

I felt tired and calm enough to go to bed now. But I did not wish to.

Wait. Mother had given me another book. *The Meanings of Flowers.* Reaching for it, I consulted the index, then looked up *chrysanthemum*.

"The bestowing of chrysanthemums indicates familial attachment and, by implication, affection."

Implied affection was better than nothing.

Idly, I looked up the sweet pea blossom.

"Good-bye, and thank you for a lovely time. A gift made upon departure."

Departure.

Next, I looked up thistles.

"Defiance."

Grimly I smiled.

So. Mum had left a message after all. Departure and defiance in the Japanese vase. In her airy sitting room with a hundred watercolours on the wall.

Watercolours of flowers.

I blinked, smiling wider. "Enola," I whispered to myself, "that's it."

"My" chrysanthemums. Mums that Mum had painted.

And framed, and displayed on the wall of her sitting room.

I knew.

Without an inkling how anything could be "in" a mum painting or what it might be, I knew that I had understood rightly, and I knew that I must go and see. This very moment. At the darkest hour of night. When no one else, especially not my brother Mycroft, would know.

Girls are supposed to play with dolls. Over the years, well-meaning adults had provided me with various dolls. I detested dolls, pulling their heads off when I could, but now I had finally found a use for them. Inside a yellow-haired doll's hollow cranium, I had hidden the key to my mother's rooms. It took me only a moment to retrieve it.

Then, lowering the wick of the oil lamp and carrying my candle with me, I softly opened my bedroom door.

My mother's door stood on the opposite end of the hallway from mine, and directly across from the guest room.

Where my brother Mycroft lay sleeping.

I hoped he was sleeping.

I hoped he was quite a sound sleeper.

Barefoot, with candlestick in one hand and my precious key in the other, I tiptoed down the hallway.

Issuing from behind Mycroft's closed bedroom door came an uncouth drone rather like that of a hog lying in the sun.

Evidently my brother snored.

A good indication that he was indeed asleep.

Excellent.

As silently as possible I inserted and turned the key in the lock of my mother's door. Still, the bolt snicked. And, as I turned the knob, the latch clicked.

A snort interrupted the rhythm of Mycroft's snoring.

Looking at his bedchamber door over my shoulder, I froze.

I heard some wallowing sounds, as if he were turning over. His bedstead creaked. Then he snored on.

Slipping into Mum's private parlour and closing the door behind me, I breathed out.

Lifting the candle, I looked up at the walls.

So many watercolours my mother had painted of so many different sorts of flowers.

I searched the four walls, straining my eyes to see the pictures in the wan candlelight. At last I found a rendition of chrysanthemums, russet and gold, like the ones in my cipher book.

Standing on tiptoe, I could just reach the bottom of the frame—a fragile one, carved like the furniture in my mother's room to resemble sticks of bamboo, their ends crossed and projecting. Gently I lifted the frame, coaxing its wire off the nail to take it down. I carried it to the tea table, where I set my candle beside it and studied it.

Enola, look in my chrysanthemums.

Often enough I had seen Mum frame her pictures. The frame itself came first, facedown on a table. Then the glass, very clean. Then a kind of inner frame cut out of thick tinted paper. To this the top edge of the watercolour was lightly gummed. Then a backing of thin wood painted white. Tiny nails driven edgewise into the frame held everything in place, and finally Mother would paste brown paper over the back of the frame to hide the nails and keep out dust.

I turned the chrysanthemum picture over and looked at its brown paper.

Taking a deep breath, I pried at one corner with my fingernails, trying to peel the paper off in one piece. Instead, a long strip of brown tore away. But never mind. I saw something nestled at the bottom of the picture, between the brown paper and the wooden backing. Something folded. Something white.

A note from Mum!

A letter explaining her desertion, expressing her regrets and her affection, perhaps even inviting me to join her . . .

With my heart pounding *please, please,* and with my fingers shaking, I fished out the rectangle of crisp paper.

Trembling, I opened it.

Yes, it was a note all right, from Mum. But not the sort of note for which I hoped.

It was a Bank of England note for a hundred pounds.

More money than most common folk saw in a year.

But money was not what I wanted from my mother.

I must admit that I cried myself to sleep. But sleep I did, finally, straight through the next morning, and no one disturbed me except that Mrs. Lane came in once and woke me to ask whether I felt ill. I told her no, I was just tired, and she left. I heard her say to someone, probably her husband, in the hallway, "She's in a state of collapse, and no wonder, poor lamb."

When I awoke in the early afternoon, although very much wanting both breakfast and luncheon, I did not at once leap out of bed. Instead, I lay still for a moment and made myself consider my situation with a clear head.

Very well. While not what I had hoped for, money was something.

Mum had secretly given me a considerable sum.

Which she had gotten, no doubt, from Mycroft.
By deceitful means.

Was it proper for me to keep it?

It was not any money that Mycroft had ever *earned*. Rather, as far as I could understand, it was money that settled on him for being Father's first-born son.

It was the inheritance of a squire. Centuries worth of rent money, with more coming in every year. And why? For the sake of Ferndell Hall and its estate.

In a very real sense, the money, like the chandeliers, *did* go with the house.

Which was, or should be, Mother's house.

Legally, the money was neither Mother's nor mine. But morally—many, many times Mum had explained to me how unfair the laws were. If a woman laboured to write and publish a book, for instance, any money it earned was supposed to go to her husband. How absurd was that?

How absurd, then, would it be for me to give that hundred-pound note back to my brother Mycroft just because he had been born first?

Legalities could go jump in a lake, I decided to my satisfaction; morally, that money was mine. Mum had sacrificed and struggled to wrest it from the estate. And she had slipped it to me.

How much more might there be? She had left me many ciphers.

What did Mother mean for me to do with it?

Already, dimly, by her example I knew the answer to that question.

CHAPTER
THE
SEVENTH

FIVE WEEKS LATER, I WAS READY.

That is to say, in the eyes of Ferndell Hall I was ready to go to boarding school.

And in my own mind, I was ready for a venture of quite a different sort.

Regarding boarding school: The seamstress had arrived from London, settled herself in a long-vacant room once occupied by a lady's maid, sighed over the old treadle sewing machine, and then taken my measurements. Waist: 20 inches. Tsk. Too large. Chest: 21 inches. Tsk. Far too small. Hips: 22 inches. Tsk. Dreadfully inadequate. But all could be set right. In a fashionable publication my mother would never have allowed in Ferndell Hall, the seamstress located the following advertisement:

AMPLIFIER: Ideal Corset for perfecting thin figures. Words cannot describe its charming effect, which is unapproachable & unattainable by any other Corset in the World. Softly padded Regulators inside (with other improvements combining softness, lightness, & comfort) regulate at wearer's pleasure any desired fullness with the graceful curves of a beautifully proportioned bust. Corset sent on approval in plain parcel on receipt of remittance. Guaranteed. Money returned if not satisfied. Avoid worthless substitutes.

This device was duly ordered, and the seamstress began to produce prim, dim-coloured dresses with high whalebone-ribbed collars to strangle me, waistbands designed to choke my breathing, and skirts which, spread over half a dozen flounced silk petticoats, trailed on the floor so that I could barely walk. She proposed to sew two dresses with a 19½-inch waist, then two with a 19-inch waist, and so on to 18½ inches and smaller, in expectation that as I grew, I would diminish.

Meanwhile, increasingly terse telegrams from

Sherlock Holmes reported no word of Mother. He had tracked down her old friends, her fellow artists, her Suffragist associates; he had even travelled to France to check with her distant relations, the Vernets, but all to no avail. I had begun to feel afraid for Mum again; why had the great detective not been able to locate her? Might some accident have befallen her after all? Or, even worse, some foul crime?

My thinking changed, however, upon the day the seamstress completed the first dress.

At which time I was expected to put on the Ideal Corset (which had arrived, as promised, in discreet brown paper wrappings) with frontal and lateral regulators plus, of course, a Patent Dress Improver so that never again would my back be able to rest against that of any chair I sat in. Also, I was expected to wear my hair in a chignon secured with hairpins that dug into my scalp, with a fringe of false curls across my forehead similarly skewered. As my reward, I got to put on my new dress and, in new shoes just as torturous, toddle around the hall to practise being a young lady.

That day I realised, with irrational yet complete certainty, where my mother had gone: someplace where there were no hairpins, no corsets (Ideal or Otherwise), and no Patent Dress Improvers.

Meanwhile, brother Mycroft sent a telegram reporting that all was arranged—I was to present myself at such-and-such a "finishing school" (house of horrors) on such-and-such a date—and instructing Lane to see to my getting there.

More importantly, regarding my own venture: I spent my days as much as I could in a dressing gown, keeping to my room and napping, pleading nervous prostration. Mrs. Lane, who frequently offered me calves' foot jelly and the like (small wonder invalids waste away!), grew so worried that she communicated with Mycroft, who assured her that boarding school, where I would breakfast upon oatmeal and wear wool next to my skin, would restore my health. Nevertheless, she summoned first the local apothecary, and later a Harley Street physician all the way from London, neither of whom found anything wrong with me.

Correctly enough. I was simply avoiding corsets, hairpins, tight shoes, and the like, while making up for lost sleep. No one knew that every night, after I had heard the rest of the household go to bed, I got up and worked on my cipher book through the dark hours. I enjoyed the ciphers after all, for I loved finding things, and Mum's ciphers gave me a new way to do this, first discovering the hidden meaning, then the treasure. Each cipher I unraveled led me into Mum's rooms in search of more riches she had secreted for me. Some of the ciphers I could not solve, which frustrated me so that I considered ripping the backing off of all Mum's watercolours — but that hardly seemed sporting. Also, there were many, many, too many paintings, and moreover, not all of the ciphers directed me to them.

There was, for instance, a page in my cipher book decorated with ivy trailing along a picket fence. At once, without even looking at the cipher, I stole into Mother's rooms in search of a watercolour study of ivy. I found two and ripped the backing off both without success before I rather sullenly returned to my room and faced the cipher:

AOEOLIMESOK
LNKONYDBBN

What in the world? I looked up *ivy* in *The Meanings of Flowers*. The clinging vine stood for "fidelity." Although touching, this knowledge did not help me. I scowled at the cipher for quite a while before I was able to pick out my name in the first three letters of the top line combined with the first two letters of the bottom line. Then I noticed how Mum had painted the ivy zigzagging in a rather unnatural manner up and down the picket fence. Also, the ivy grew from right to left. Rolling my eyes, I followed the same pattern and rewrote the cipher:

KNOBSBEDMYINLOOKENOLA

KNOBS BED MY IN LOOK ENOLA

Or, reading the words from right to left:

ENOLA LOOK IN MY BED KNOBS

Off I went, tiptoeing through the night, to remove the knobs from Mum's bed and discover that an astonishing amount of paper money can be stuffed inside brass bedposts.

I, in my turn, had to find clever hiding places within my bedroom so that Mrs. Lane's occasional invasions with dust-cloth would discover nothing.

My curtain rods, made of brass like Mother's bed, with knobs on the ends, served the purpose.

And all of this had to be done before the Lanes rose at dawn.

Altogether, my nights were far more active and satisfactory than my days.

I did not ever find what I most desired—any note of farewell, affectionate regard, or explanation from Mum. But truly, at this point, not much explanation was needed. I knew that she had practised her deceptions for my sake, at least in part. And I knew that the money she had so cleverly slipped to me was meant to give me freedom.

Thanks to Mum, therefore, it was in a surprisingly hopeful, if nervous, state of mind that, one sunny morning in late August, I mounted to the seat of the conveyance that was to take me away from the only home I had ever known.

Lane had arranged with a local farmer for the loan of a horse and a kind of hybrid contraption, or "trap," a luggage-wagon with an upholstered seat for me and the driver. I was to travel to the railway station in comfort, if not in style.

"I hope it doesn't rain," Mrs. Lane remarked, standing in the drive to see me off.

It hadn't rained in weeks. Not since the day I had gone searching for my mother.

"Unlikely," said Lane, giving me his hand so that I could step up to my seat like a lady, one kid-gloved hand in his while the other lifted my white ruffled parasol. "There's not a cloud in the sky."

Smiling down on Lane and Mrs. Lane, I settled first my bustle, then myself, next to Dick, my driver. Just as my bustle occupied the back of the seat, Mrs. Lane had arranged my hair to occupy the back of my head, as was the fashion, so that my hat, rather like a beribboned straw dinner plate, tilted forward over my eyes. I wore a taupe suit I had chosen carefully for its nondescript, indeed ugly colour, its 19½-inch waistband, full skirt, and concealing jacket. Beneath the jacket I had left the skirt's waistband unbuttoned so that I could corset myself as lightly as possible, almost comfortably. I could breathe.

As would be needful very soon.

"You look every inch a lady, Miss Enola," said Lane, standing back. "You'll be a credit to Ferndell Hall, I'm sure."

Little did he know.

"We'll miss you," quavered Mrs. Lane, and for a moment my heart reproached me, for I saw tears on her soft old face.

"Thank you," I said rather stiffly, starching myself against my own emotion. "Dick, drive on."

All the way to the gate I stared at the horse's ears. My brother Mycroft had hired men to "clean up" the lawn of the estate, and I did not want to see it with my wild rosebushes cut down.

"Good-bye, Miss Enola, and good luck," said the lodge-keeper as he opened the gates for us.

"Thank you, Cooper."

As the horse trotted through Kineford, I sighed and allowed my glance to roam, taking a farewell look at the butcher's shop, the greengrocer's shop, black-beamed, whitewashed thatched cottages, public house, post and telegraph office, constabulary, more Tudor cottages with tiny windows scowling under their heavy straw forelocks, the inn, the smithy, the vicarage, the granite chapel with its mossy slate roof, headstones tilting this way and that in the graveyard—

I let us trot almost past before I said suddenly, as

if I had just that moment thought of it, "Dick, stop. I wish to say good-bye to my father."

He pulled the horse to a halt. "What was that, Miss Enola?"

When dealing with Dick, full and simple explanations were necessary. "I wish to visit my father's grave," I told him one patient word at a time, "and say a prayer for him in the chapel."

Poor Father, he would not have desired such prayers. As a logician and an unbeliever, Mum had once told me, he had not desired a funeral; his request had been for cremation, but after his demise, his wishes had been overruled for fear that Kineford might never recover from the scandal.

In his slow, worried way Dick said, "I'm to drive you to the railway station, miss."

"There is plenty of time. You can have a pint at the public house while you're waiting for me."

"Oh! Aye." He turned the horse, backtracked, and drew up at the door of the chapel. We sat for a moment before he remembered his manners, but then he secured the reins, got down, and came around to my side to help me descend.

"Thank you," I told him as I withdrew my gloved

93

hand from his grubby fist. "Come back for me in ten minutes."

Nonsense; I knew he'd be half an hour or more in the public house.

"Yes, miss." He touched his cap.

He drove away, and amid a swirl of skirts I minced into the chapel.

As I had expected and hoped, I found it unoccupied. After scanning the empty pews, I grinned, tossed my parasol into the castoff-clothing-for-the-poor box, hoisted my skirts above my knees, and dashed for the back door.

And out into the sunlit graveyard.

Down a twisting path worn between the tottering headstones I ran, keeping the chapel between me and any witness who might be passing upon the village street. When I reached the hedge at the bottom of the chapel grounds, I leapt more than climbed the stile, turned right, ran a bit farther, and yes, indeed, yes! There waited my bicycle, hidden in the hedge, where I had left it yesterday. Or rather, yesternight. In the small hours, by the light of a nearly full moon.

On the bicycle were mounted two containers, a basket in front and a box in back, both packed full of sandwiches, pickles, hard-boiled eggs, water flask, bandaging in case of accident, tyre repair kit, knickerbockers, my comfortable old black boots, toothbrush, and such.

On my person, also, were mounted two containers, hidden beneath the taupe suit, one in front and one in back. The one in front was a quite unique bust enhancer that I had secretly hand-sewn for myself out of materials purloined from Mum's wardrobe. For the container in back, I had devised a dress improver of like sort.

Why, leaving home, had my mother worn a bustle, yet left its horsehair stuffing behind?

The answer seemed obvious to me: in order to conceal in the dress improver's place the baggage necessary for running away.

And I, being blessed with a flat chest, had carried her example a step further. My various and proper regulators, enhancers, and improvers remained in Ferndell Hall—stuffed up my chimney, actually. In their places upon my person I wore cloth containers—baggage, in effect—filled with unmentionables wrapped around bundles of bank notes. In addition, I had folded a carefully chosen spare dress and secured it to my back between my petticoats, where it perfectly filled my train. In the pockets of my suit I had a handkerchief, a cake of soap, comb and hairbrush, my now-precious booklet of ciphers, smelling salts, energy-sustaining candies ... indeed, I bore a steamer trunk's worth of essentials.

Hopping onto my bicycle, letting my petticoats and skirts modestly drape my ankles, I pedalled off across country.

A good cyclist does not need a road. I would follow the farm lanes and pasturelands for the time being. The ground was baked hard as iron; I would leave no tracks.

By tomorrow, I imagined, my brother the great detective Sherlock Holmes would be attempting to locate a missing sister as well as a missing mother.

He would expect me to flee from him. Therefore, I would not. I would flee towards him.

He lived in London. So did Mycroft. On that account, and also because it was the world's largest and most dangerous city, it was the last place on earth either of them would expect me to venture.

Therefore, I would go there.

They would expect me to disguise myself as a boy. Very likely they had heard about my knickerbockers, and anyway, in Shakespeare and other works of fiction, runaway girls always disguised themselves as boys.

Therefore, I would not.

I would disguise myself as the last thing my brothers would think I could, having met me as a plain beanpole of a child in a frock that barely covered my knees.

I would disguise myself as a grown woman.

And then I would set about finding my mother.

CHAPTER
THE
EIGHTH

I COULD HAVE PEDALLED STRAIGHT INTO London by the main road, but that would never do. Too many people would see me. No, my plan for getting to London was simply—and, I hoped, illogically—to have no plan. If I myself did not know what exactly I was doing, then how could my brothers guess?

They would hypothesise, of course; they would say, "Mother took her to Bath, so perhaps she has gone there," or "In her room there is a book on Wales, with pencil markings on the map; perhaps she has gone there." (I hoped they would find the book, which I had placed in the dollhouse as a false clue. *The Meanings of Flowers,* however, too large to carry with me, I had hidden among hundreds of other stout volumes in the library downstairs.) Mycroft and Sherlock would apply inductive reasoning; therefore, I reasoned, I must trust to chance. I would let the land show me the way eastward, choosing the stoniest ground or whatever would show my tyre marks the least.

It did not matter where I found myself at the end of that day, or the next. I would dine upon bread and cheese, I would sleep in the open like a Gypsy, and eventually, wandering along, I would encounter a railway line. By following it one way or the other, I would find a station, and so long as it was *not* Chaucerlea (where my brothers would surely inquire for me), any station in England would do, for all railways ran to London.

So much for a seventeen-inch waist, oatmeal for breakfast and wool next to the skin, matrimonial prospects, the accomplishments of a young lady, et cetera.

Such were my happy thoughts as I pedalled across a cow pasture, along a grassy lane, then onto open moorland, and away from the countryside I knew.

In the blue sky overhead, larks sang like my heart.

As I kept to byways and avoided villages, not too

many people saw me. An occasional farmer looked up from his turnip field, unsurprised by the sight of a gentlewoman upon her bicycle; such cycling enthusiasts had grown increasingly common. Indeed, I met with just another such beige-clad figure upon a gravel wagon track, and we nodded in passing. She looked all of a glow from the heat and the exercise. Horses sweat, you know, and men perspire, whereas ladies glow. I am sure I looked all of a glow also. Indeed, I could feel all-of-a-glow trickling down my sides beneath my corset, the steel ribs of which jabbed me under the arms most annoyingly.

By the time the sun stood overhead, I felt quite ready to stop for luncheon, all the more so as I had not slept the night before. Seated under a spreading elm tree, upon a cushion of moss, I badly wanted to lie down and pillow my head there for a while. But after I had eaten, I forced myself to get back upon the bicycle and pedal onward, for I knew I must get as far away as possible before the pursuit began.

That afternoon, aptly enough considering my thoughts of Gypsies, I met with a caravan of the nomad folk in their brightly painted round-topped house-wagons. Most gentry despised Gypsies, but Mother had allowed them to camp sometimes upon the Ferndell estate, and as a child I had been fascinated by them. Even now I halted my bicycle to watch them pass, gazing eagerly upon their many-coloured horses prancing and tossing their heads despite the heat, with the drivers needing to hold them in more than urge them forward. And I waved to the travellers in the wagons without fear, for of all people on earth Gypsies were the least likely to speak of me to the police. The men darkly ignored me, but some of the bare-headed, bare-necked, bare-armed women waved back, and all of the ragged children waved and squealed and called out, begging. Shameless, dirty, thieving lot, Mrs. Lane would have called them, and I suppose she was right. Yet if I'd been carrying pennies in my pocket, I would have thrown some to them.

Also that afternoon on a country road I met a travelling peddler, his wagon hung round with tin-ware and umbrellas and baskets and sea sponges and birdcages and washboards and all manner of trifles. I stopped him and had him show me everything in his stock, from copper kettles to tortoise-shell combs for the back of the hair, in order to disguise my purpose before I bought the one thing I really needed: a carpet-bag.

Laying it across my handle-bars, I pedalled on.

I saw other wayfarers, on foot and in conveyances ranging from coach-and-four to donkey-carts, but my memories become faulty as my weariness blurred the day. By the time night fell, every part of my person ached, and I felt fagged as never before in my life. Walking now upon turf cropped to the roots by sheep, pushing my bicycle and leaning upon it, I struggled up a low, limestone-studded hill on top of which stood a grove of beeches. Once I reached the concealment of the trees, I let my bicycle fall where it would, while I myself collapsed in dirt and last year's leaves, my spirits as low with evening as they had been high with morning, for I wondered: Would I find strength to get on that bicycle again tomorrow?

I could sleep where I was. Unless . . . for the first time I thought: What if it rained?

My plan not to plan seemed more foolish with every panting breath I drew.

After I had despaired for a while, I managed to stagger up and, in the concealing darkness, take off my hat, hairpins, and the baggage I carried on my person, along with my tormenting corset. Too weary even to think of food, I folded to the ground again and, wearing petticoats and my much-soiled taupe suit as my only covering, fell asleep within moments.

So nocturnal had my habits become, however, that sometime late at night I awoke.

No longer the least bit sleepy, I felt famished.

But there was no moon tonight. The sky had clouded over. It might indeed rain. And without moonlight or even starlight, I could not see to find myself the food I had packed in the box on the bicycle. Nor could I see to find, for the sake of light, the tin of matches I had stupidly left in the same place. I would consider myself fortunate if I stumbled upon the bicycle at all.

"Curses," I muttered naughtily, feeling beech twigs scratch my face and catch at my clothing as I lurched to my feet.

But the next moment I forgot about food. I stood staring, for at no great distance I saw lights.

Gas lamps. Glimpsed between the trunks of the hilltop trees, they twinkled in the distance like earthbound stars.

A village. I had come up one side of the hill not knowing, and too weary to realise, that a village lay on the other side.

A town, rather, being large enough to have gas laid on.

A town with, perhaps, a railway station?

And even as I thought it, there came floating to my ears, across the dark of night, a train whistle's long tenor call.

Very, very early the next morning, I stole out of the beech woods — so early, I hoped, that few if any folk would catch sight of me. Not that I was afraid anyone would recognise me. It was just that it would look a bit odd for a well-dressed widow, on foot, with a carpet-bag, to emerge from such primitive lodging.

Yes, a widow. Head to toe, I wore the black garb of mourning I had taken from my mother's closet. The costume, by indicating that I had been married, added a decade or more to my age, yet allowed me to wear my comfortable old black boots, which would not be noticed, and my hair in a simple bun, which I could manage. Best of all, it made me nearly unrecognisable. Hanging from the brim of my black felt hat, a dense black veil enveloped my entire head, so that I looked rather as if I intended to raid a bee-hive. Black kid-leather gloves covered my hands —

I had made sure of this detail, as I lacked a wedding ring—and dull black silk covered me from my chin to my black-booted toes.

Ten years ago, Mum had been thinner, so her dress fit me nicely with my corset barely tightened at all; indeed, no corset would have been necessary if it were not to support my improvised baggage in the necessary areas. What I'd packed on the bicycle I now carried in the carpet-bag or in my pockets. Disliking to dangle a reticule, my mother had provided all her dresses with ample pockets for handkerchief, lemon drops, shillings and pence, et cetera. Blessings be upon the stubbornly independent head of my mother, who was also the one who had taught me to ride a bicycle. I regretted having to abandon that faithful mechanical steed to the beech woods, but I most certainly did not regret abandoning my ugly taupe suit.

In the grey half-light of daybreak, I stole downhill along a hedge to a lane. Very stiff from yesterday's exertions, I realised that my aches and pains were actually a blessing: they forced me to walk slowly. Thus, at a ladylike gait in keeping with my disguise, I made my way along the lane to a gravelled road, and so into the town.

Dawn had progressed to a dull sunrise, threatening rain. Shopkeepers were just opening their shutters, the ice-man was hitching up his sway-backed nag to make his rounds, a yawning maid threw a bucket of something unspeakable into the gutter, a ragged woman swept a street crossing. Newsboys heaved stacks of the morning edition towards the curb. A match-seller sitting at a corner — a beggar, really — cried, "Let there be light; a match for the gentleman?" Some of those who passed by were indeed gentlemen in top-hats, others workmen in flannels and caps, yet others nearly as ragged as himself, but he cried "gentleman" to them all. He made no attempt to sell a match to me, of course, for ladies did not smoke.

BELVIDERE TONSORIUM declared gold letters painted on the glass of a door beside a red-and-white spiral-striped pole. Ah, I had heard of a town called Belvidere, satisfactorily distant from Kineford. Looking about me, I saw SAVINGS BANK OF BELVIDERE carved upon the stone lintel of a stately building nearby. Very good; I had achieved my goal. *Well done*, I thought, picking my way between horse droppings, *for a mere girl of limited cranial capacity.*

"Onions, potatoes, parsnips!" called a man pushing a barrow.

"Fresh carnation for the gent's buttonhole!" cried a shawled woman offering flowers from a basket.

"Shocking kidnapping! Read all about it!" bellowed a newsboy.

Kidnapping?

"Viscount Tewksbury snatched from Basilwether Hall!"

I did indeed want to read all about it, but first I wanted to find the railway station.

With this in mind, I followed a top-hatted, frock-coated, kid-gloved gentleman who was positioning a fresh carnation upon his lapel. Formally dressed, perhaps he was going to the city for the day.

Affirming my hypothesis, soon I heard the rumble of an approaching engine crescendo to a roar that shook the pavement beneath my boots. Then I could see the peaked roof and turrets of the station, with the clock in its tower reading just half past seven, and I could hear the shriek and whine of brakes as the train pulled in.

Whether my unwitting escort travelled to London, I will never know, for as we approached the station platform, my attention was all taken up by the scene unfolding there.

A gawking crowd had gathered. A number of constables formed a line to keep the onlookers back, while yet more officials in blue uniform strode forward to meet the newly arrived train, an engine pulling a single car importantly labeled POLICE EXPRESS. Out of this stepped several men in travelling cloaks. These swept the ground impressively enough, but the ear-flaps of the matching cloth caps done up in bows atop their heads looked like little bunny ears, quite silly, I thought as I started to edge through the crowd towards the ticket window of the station.

As if I had walked into a pot on the boil, all around me bubbled excited voices.

"It's Scotland Yard, right enough. Plainclothes detectives."

"I heard they sent for Sherlock Holmes, too—"

Oh, my goodness. Halting, eagerly I listened.

"—but he won't come, he's called away by family—"

The speaker passed by, confound it, and I heard no more of my brother, although other babble aplenty.

"My cousin's the second assistant upstairs maid at the big house—"

"The duchess has gone clean out of her head, folk say."

"—and she says they—"

"And the duke is fit to be tied."

"Old Pickering at the bank says they're still waiting for a ransom demand."

"Who'd want the boy if not for ransom?"

Hmm. It would seem that the "Shocking Kidnapping!" had taken place close by. Indeed, watching the detectives pile into quite a lovely landau, I saw them being trotted off towards a green park not far beyond the railway station. Above the trees rose the grey Gothic towers of—from the talk around me—Basilwether Hall.

How interesting.

But first things first. I must purchase a ticket—

However, according to the large schedule posted upon the station wall, there would be no lack of trains to London. Every hour or so all day and into the evening.

"Duke's son gone missing! Read all about it!" shrieked a newsboy standing beneath the schedule.

While no believer in providence, I had to wonder

how chance had placed me here, on this scene of crime, and my brother the great detective elsewhere. My thoughts became unruly, and their lure irresistible. Abandoning my attempt to reach the ticket window, I bought a newspaper instead.

CHAPTER
THE
NINTH

AT A TEA-SHOP BESIDE BELVIDERE STATION, I sat at a corner table, facing the wall in order to lift my veil. I needed to do this for two purposes: to breakfast upon tea and scones, and to look at young Viscount Tewksbury Basilwether's photographic likeness.

Occupying nearly half the front page of the newspaper, a formal studio portrait showed the boy dressed in—heavens have mercy, I hoped he wasn't made to wear velvet and frills every day—but how else might he go about with his fair hair, rendered artistic by the curling tongs, hanging to his shoulders? All too apparently his mother had fallen in love with *Little Lord Fauntleroy*, wretched book responsible for the agonies of a generation of well-born boys. Got up in the height of Fauntleroy fashion, little Lord Tewksbury wore patent leather buckle slippers, white stockings, black velvet knee pants with satin bows at the sides, and a satin sash under his black velvet jacket with its flowing white lace cuffs and collar. He stared at the camera with no expression whatsoever on his face, but I thought I saw a trace of hardness around his jaw.

DUKE'S HEIR OF TENDER YEARS HORRIFICALLY MISSING

screamed the headline.

Reaching for a second scone, I read:

A scene of the most alarming implications unfolded early Wednesday morning at Basilwether Hall, ancestral home of the Dukes of Basilwether, near the thriving town of Belvidere, when an under-gardener noticed that one of the French doors of the billiards room had been broken into. The household staff then being alerted, next discovered that the lock of the room's interior door had been forced, the woodwork showing the marks of a vicious knife. Naturally fearful of burglary, the butler checked the silverware pantry and discovered nothing missing. Nor were the plate and candelabra of the dining room disturbed, or the innumerable valuable contents of the drawing-room, the gallery, the library, or anywhere else in Basilwether Hall's extensive premises. Indeed no further doors had been forced downstairs. It was not until the upstairs maids commenced carrying the customary ewers of hot water to the ducal family's quarters for their matutinal ablutions, that Viscount Tewksbury, Marquess of Basilwether's chamber door was found standing ajar. His furnishings, strewn about the room, bore mute witness to a desperate struggle, and of his noble personage there was no sign. The Viscount, Lord Basilwether's heir and, indeed, his only son, a mere twelve years of age—

"Twelve?" I exclaimed, incredulous.

"What is that, madam?" asked the hostess behind me.

"Ah, nothing." Hastily I lowered the newspaper to the table and my veil to cover my face. "I thought he was younger." Much younger, in his curled tresses and storybook suit. Twelve! Why, the boy should be wearing a sturdy woollen jacket and knickers, an Eton collar with a tie, and a decent, manly haircut—

Thoughts, I realised, all too similar to those of my brother Sherlock upon meeting me.

"Poor lost Lord Tewksbury, you mean? Aye, his mother has kept him a baby. One hears she's wild with grief, unfortunate lady."

I pushed back my chair, left a halfpenny on the table, exited the tea-shop and, after entrusting my carpet-bag to a porter at the railway station, walked towards Basilwether Park.

This would be far better than searching for bright pebbles and birds' nests. Something truly valuable was to be found, and I wanted to find it. And I believed perhaps I could. I knew where Lord Tewksbury might be. I just knew, although I did not know how to prove it. All the way up the long drive lined with giant poplar trees I walked in a kind of trance, imagining where he might have gone.

The first gates stood open, but at the second gates, a lodge-keeper stopped me, his duty being to keep out the idle curious, newspaper reporters, and the like. He asked me, "Your name, ma'am?"

"Enola Holmes," I said without thinking.

Instantly I felt so inexcusably stupid, I wanted to expire on the spot. Running away, I had of course chosen a new name for myself: Ivy Meshle. "Ivy" for fidelity—to my mother. "Meshle" as a kind of cipher. Take "Holmes," divide it into *hol mes*, reverse it into *mes hol*, *Meshol*, then spell it the way it was pronounced: Meshle. It would be a rare soul who could connect me with anyone else in England ("Are you related to the Sussex Meshles of Tottering Heath?"), much less to anyone named Holmes. Ivy Meshle. So clever. Ivy Meshle! And now like an imbecile I had told this lodge-keeper, "Enola Holmes."

Judging by his blank face, the name meant nothing to him. Yet. If any foxhunt after me had begun, the view-halloo had not yet reached this area or this man. "And your business here, Mrs., um, Holmes?" he asked.

Having been a fool, I decided, I might as well make the most of it. I said, "As Mr. Sherlock Holmes could not himself attend to this matter, he asked me to come and have a look about."

The lodge-keeper's brows lurched, and he blurted, "You're related to the *detective*, ma'am?"

"Indeed," I replied, my tone quelling, and I swept past him, marching into Basilwether Park.

The hall, rising before me at the circular end of the drive, would have held ten of Ferndell—but I did not approach its wide marble steps or its pillared doors. My interest did not lie in that noble residence, nor in the formal gardens all around it, studded with topiaries and glittering with well-disciplined roses. Veering away from the drive, I walked across an expanse of lawn towards Basilwether Park proper, that is to say, the woodlands surrounding the hall and gardens.

Not forest. Woodlands. Stepping beneath the trees, expecting to meet a few thickets, a patch of moss or two, some kindred brambles, I found instead soft grass trimmed short enough to play croquet upon.

A tame place, this. Walking along, I discovered no interesting hollows, dells, or grottos. Basilwether Hall's estate was flat and featureless. How disappointing, I thought as I emerged onto lawn again. The only possibility might be —

"Mrs. Holmes!" cried a wild soprano voice, and I turned to see the distraught mother, the duchess, hurtling towards me. I knew it was she because of the richness of her day dress, the heavy braiding and embroidery on her silver-grey capelet over a gown of shirred mauve drawn back from a pleated underskirt of rose-grey satin. But there was nothing of richness in the tears stark on her staring face, and nothing of the nobility in the way she flew at me between the trees like a bloodied swan, wings of nearly white hair falling out from under her hat to flap about her shoulders.

A pair of frightened-looking maids came hurrying up behind her. In their aprons and white lace caps, they must have run straight out of the house after her. "Your Grace," they cried, coaxing, "Your Grace, please come in, do, and have a cup of tea. Please, it's going to rain." But the duchess seemed not to hear them.

"Mrs. Holmes." I felt her bare hands trembling as she grasped at me. "You are a woman, with a woman's heart; tell me, who could have done this evil thing? Where could my Tewky be? What am I to *do*?"

Holding her quivering hands in both my own, I felt grateful for the heavy veil hiding my dismayed face, grateful for the gloves that separated my warm flesh from hers, so cold. "Have courage, um, Your Grace, and, um . . ." I fumbled for words. "Be of good hope." Then I could blunder on. "Let me ask you this: was there anywhere . . ." The way she doted on him, she might have spied or surmised. "A place on the grounds where your son would go to be alone?"

"To be alone?" Her swollen, red-rimmed eyes blinked at me utterly without comprehension. "Whatever do you mean?"

"Sheerest nonsense," proclaimed a resonant alto voice behind me. "This insignificant widow knows nothing. *I* will find the lost child, Your Grace."

Turning, I found myself looking at the most extraordinary woman, even taller than I and far bulkier, shockingly hatless and uncoifed. Her wiry hair spread about her head, shoulder to shoulder, for all the world as if she were a white lamp and her hair a red shade: not chestnut, not auburn, but true red, almost scarlet, the colour of a poppy blossom, while her eyes glared out of her rice-powdered face as sooty dark as a poppy's black heart. So arresting were her hair and face that I barely noticed her clothing. I have only a vague impression of cotton, perhaps from Egypt or India, in some barbaric crimson pattern, petalled around her massive body as wildly as the poppy-hued hair around her face.

The duchess gasped, "Madame Laelia? Oh, you've come, as I begged you to, Madame Laelia!"

Madame what? Madame Spiritualist Medium, I surmised, this being one role in which women, the morally and spiritually superior gender, commanded greater respect than men. But such characters—or charlatans, as my mother would have it—evoked the spirits of the dead. And surely the duchess most fervidly hoped her son was not one of those, so what was this oversized female doing—

"Madame Laelia Sibyl de Papaver, Astral Perditorian, at your service," the statuesque one proclaimed. "Whatever is lost, I can surely find, for the spirits go everywhere, know all, see all, and they are my friends."

The duchess now seized upon this woman's large yellow-gloved hands, while I, like the two meek maids, stood there with my mouth airing, thunderstruck. But, in my case, not by this woman's grotesque appearance. Nor by her talk of spirits. While I wanted to believe that I would somehow persevere after my corporeal body was gone, I imagined that if it were so, I would have better things to do than to knock on furniture, ring bells, and shake tables. Nor did the word *astral* impress me. Of all that Madame Laelia Sibyl de Papaver had said, it was a single word that rendered me motionless and speechless.

That word: *Perðitorian.*

From the Latin *perðitus,* meaning "lost."

Perditorian: one who divines that which is lost.

But . . . but how dare she, with all her blather of spirits, title herself so nobly? Knower of the lost, wise woman of the lost, finder of the lost: That was *my* calling.

I was a perditorian. Or I would be. Not astral. Professional. The world's first professional, logical, scientific perditorian.

All in one gasping breath of inspiration, I knew this as surely as I knew my real name was Holmes.

I scarcely noticed how the maids escorted the duchess and Madame Laelia into the hall, perhaps for tea, perhaps for a séance; I did not care. Back in the woodlands that encircled Basilwether Park, I walked at random, oblivious to the drizzle that had begun to fall, my thoughts running wild with excitement, building upon my original scheme to find Mum.

That plan remained simple: Upon arriving in London, I would hail a cab, tell the driver to take me to a respectable hotel, and have dinner and a good night's sleep. Staying at the hotel until I found suitable lodgings, I would set up bank accounts—no, first I would go to Fleet Street and place encrypted "personals" in the publications I knew Mum read. Wherever she was, would she not continue to read her favourite journals? Of course. I would wait until Mum replied. Just wait.

That would suffice, if—as I often found it necessary to reassure myself—if indeed Mum was alive and well.

In any event, wait was all I could do.

Or so I had thought. But now, now that I had found my calling in life, I could do so much more. Let my brother Sherlock be The World's Only Private Consulting Detective all he liked; I would be The World's Only Private Consulting Perditorian. As such, I could associate with professional women who met in their own tea-rooms around London— women who might know Mum!—and with the detectives of Scotland Yard—where Sherlock had already filed an inquiry concerning Mum—and with other dignitaries, and also perhaps with disreputable persons who had information to sell, and—oh, the possibilities. I was born to be a perditorian. A finder of loved ones lost. And—

And I ought to stop dreaming about it and start doing it. Right now.

The only possibility, as I had been thinking before I was interrupted, seemed to be perhaps a tree.

Backtracking through the boringly well-tended woodlands of Basilwether Park, I concentrated now on looking for that particular tree. It would be located not too near Basilwether Hall and its formal garden, and not too near the edge of Basilwether Park, either, but in the middle of the woods, where adult eyes would be least likely to spy. And like my refuge under the overhanging willow in Ferndell's fern dell, it had to be distinctive in some way. Different. Worthy of being a hideaway.

The thin rain had stopped, the sun had come out, and I had nearly circled the estate before I found it.

It was not one tree, actually, but four growing from a single base. Four maple seedlings had planted themselves in the same place, and all had survived to form a symmetrical cluster whose four trunks rose at a steep angle from one another, with a perfect square of space in between.

Planting one booted foot upon a gnarl and grasping a handy bough, I swung myself up to stand perhaps three feet above the ground inside the encompassing V's of the trunks, a perfect axis at the hub of a foursquare leaf-encircled universe. Delightful.

Even more delightful: I saw that someone, presumably young Lord Tewksbury, had been here also. He had hammered a large nail—a railroad spike, actually—into the trunk of one of the trees on the inside. No one walking by was likely to notice it, but there it sturdily jutted.

To hang something upon? No, a much smaller nail would have served that purpose. I knew what this spike was for.

To set one's foot upon. To climb.

Oh, glorious day, to climb a tree once again after so many weeks of ladylike confinement . . . But oh, consternation, for what if anyone observed me? A widow lady in a tree?

I looked all around, saw no one, and decided to chance it. Ridding myself of my hat and veil, concealing them in the leaves overhead, I hoisted my skirt and petticoats into a bunch above my knees, securing it with hatpins. Then, setting my foot upon the spike and seizing a branch, up I went.

Twigs snagged my hair, but I didn't care. Except for the usual jabs in the face, it was as easy as climbing a ladder—a good thing, as my sore limbs protested every inch of the way. But Lord Tewksbury, happily for me, had driven railroad spikes wherever no maple boughs presented themselves. Brilliant lad, this young viscount. No doubt he had obtained the spikes from the tracks that ran past his father's estate. I hoped no trains had derailed on his account.

After I had climbed twenty feet or so, I stopped to see where I was going. I tilted my head back—

Good heavens.

He had built a platform in the tree.

A structure not at all visible from the ground when the trees were in leaf, but from my perch I could admire it clearly enough: a square framework made of scraps of unpainted lumber, set between the four maples. Supporting beams ran from trunk to trunk, wedged into place on tree limbs or else secured with cord lashed around the corners. Planks lay across the beams to form a crude sort of floor. I imagined him scavenging that wood from cellars or stable lofts or goodness knew where, dragging it here, maybe creeping out at night to lift it into the tree with a rope and set it in place.

And all the time his mother applying the curling tongs to his hair, and clothing him in satin, velvet, and lace. Heaven have mercy.

In one corner of the platform he had left an opening by which to enter. As I popped my head through, my respect for young Lord Tewksbury only increased. He had suspended a square of canvas, perhaps a wagon cover, as a roof over his hideaway. In the corners he had placed saddle-blankets presumably "borrowed" from the stable, folded to serve as cushions to sit upon. Into the four tree trunks he had driven nails from which hung loops of knotted cord, pictures of boats, a metal whistle, all sorts of interesting things.

I crawled in to look.

But at once my attention was arrested by a shocking sight in the middle of the plank floor.

Scraps, fragments, rag-tag bits cut and torn so

dreadfully that it took me a moment to recognise what they were: black velvet, white lace, baby-blue satin. Remains of what had once been clothing.

And atop that heap of ruins, hair. Long, curled locks of golden hair.

He must have shorn his head to stubble.

After ripping his finery to shreds.

Viscount Tewksbury had entered this refuge. Of his own free will. No kidnapper would have or could have brought him here.

And by the looks of things, Viscount Tewksbury had left this hideaway as he had come, of his own free will. But no longer to be Viscount Tewksbury, Marquess of Basilwether.

CHAPTER THE TENTH

ON THE GROUND AGAIN, WITH MY SKIRTS down where they belonged, my black hat pinned in place to cover my unkempt head, and my veil pulled down to conceal my face, I walked blindly. I did not know what to do.

Around one gloved forefinger I twisted a lock of long, blond, curled hair. The rest I had left where I had found it. I imagined the wild birds taking it away strand by strand to line their nests.

I thought of the mute, enraged message the runaway boy had left in his secret sanctuary.

I thought of the tears I had seen on his mother's face. Poor lady.

But equally, poor lad. Made to wear velvet and lace. Almost as bad as a steel-ribbed corset.

Not at all incidentally, I thought of myself. I, Enola, on the run just like young Lord Tewksbury, except that it was to be hoped he'd had the sense to change his name. Fool that I'd been, coming here as Enola Holmes, I had put myself in jeopardy. I needed to get away.

Still, I must reassure the unfortunate duchess—

No. No, I should leave Basilwether Park as quickly as possible, before—

"Mrs. Holmes?"

Stiffening, I found myself on the carriage-drive directly in front of Basilwether Hall, uncertain whether to advance or retreat, when a voice called to me from above.

"Mrs. Holmes!"

Hiding the lock of blond hair in the palm of one hand, I turned to see a man in a travelling cloak hurrying down the marble steps towards me. One of the detectives from London.

"Excuse me for presuming upon your acquaintance," he said when he stood before me, "but the lodge-keeper informed us you were here, and I wondered . . ." He was a small, weasel-like man, hardly the muscular sort one expected of a police department, yet fearsome in the way his beady eyes peered at me, like shiny black ladybugs trying to crawl right through my veil. In a rather high-pitched voice he went on, "I am an acquaintance of Mr. Sherlock Holmes. My name is Lestrade."

"How do you do." I did not offer to shake hands.

"Very well, thank you. I must say it is an unexpected pleasure to meet you." His tone hinted for information. He knew my name was Enola Holmes. He could see that I was a widow. Therefore he titled me Mrs., but if I were merely related by marriage to the Holmes family, he must have been thinking, why would Sherlock send me in his stead? "I must say Holmes has never mentioned you to me."

"Indeed." Politely I nodded. "And have you discussed your family with him?"

"No! Er, I mean, there has not been occasion."

"Of course not." My tone remained, I hope, bland, but my thoughts twittered like a chaffinch. This snoop would tell Sherlock he had met me, and under what circumstances, at his first opportunity. No, worse! As an inspector for Scotland Yard, at any minute he might receive a wire concerning me. I had to get away before that happened. He seemed suspicious of me already. I had to distract Inspector Lestrade from inspecting *me*.

Opening my gloved hand, I uncoiled a lock of fair hair and held it out to him.

"Regarding Lord Tewksbury," I said in a commanding manner mimicking that of my famous brother, "he has not been kidnapped." I waved aside the inspector's attempt to protest. "He has taken matters into his own hands; he has run away. You would, too, if you were dressed like a doll in a velvet suit. He wants to go to sea on a boat. A ship, I mean." In the young viscount's hideaway I had seen pictures of steamships, clipper ships, all sorts of seafaring vessels. "In particular, he admires that huge monstrosity, the one that looks like a floating cattle trough with sails on top and paddle-wheels on the sides, what is its name? The one that laid the transatlantic cable?"

But Inspector Lestrade's gaze remained riveted upon the blond, curling tresses in my hand. He babbled, "What . . . where . . . how do you deduce . . ."

"The *Great Eastern*." At last I remembered the name of the world's largest ship. "You will find Lord Tewksbury at a seaport, probably the docks of London, in all likelihood applying for a berth as a seaman or a cabin boy, as he has been practising tying sailors' knots. He has cut his hair. He must have gotten some common clothing somehow, perhaps from the stable boys; you might want to question them. After such a transformation, I imagine no one at the station recognised him if he went by train."

"But the broken door! The forced lock!"

"He did that so that you would search for a kidnapper rather than a runaway. Rather mean of him," I admitted, "to worry his mother so." This thought made me feel better about telling what I knew. "Perhaps you could give Her Grace this." I thrust the lock of hair at Inspector Lestrade. "Although truly, I do not know whether it will help her feel better or make her feel worse."

Gawking at me, Inspector Lestrade seemed barely to know what he was doing as his right hand rose to accept the tresses of a duke's son.

"But—but where did you find this?" With his other hand he reached for me as if to grip me by the elbow and draw me into Basilwether Hall. Stepping back, away from his grasp, I became aware of a third party to the conversation. At the top of the marble stairway, looming amid balustrades and Grecian columns, Madame Laelia watched and listened.

I lowered my voice to answer Inspector Lestrade quite softly. "In the first floor, so to speak, of a maple tree with four trunks." I pointed in its direction, and as he turned to look, I walked away, rather more quickly than a lady should, down the drive towards the gates.

"Mrs. Holmes!" he shouted after me.

Without altering the rhythm of my pace or looking back, I lifted one hand in a polite but dismissive wave, imitating the way my brother had waggled his walking stick at me. Restraining an impulse to run, I kept walking.

When I had passed through the gates, I breathed out.

Not having ridden in a train before, I was surprised to find the second-class passenger car divided into little parlours for four people each, with leather seats facing each other as in a carriage. I had imagined something more open, like an omnibus. But not so: A conductor led me down a narrow aisle, opened a door, and willy-nilly I found myself compartmented with three strangers, taking the one remaining place, which faced the rear of the train.

Moments later I felt myself being carried, slowly at first but moment by moment accelerating, backwards towards London.

All too apt a position, as Inspector Lestrade had so reversed my affairs that I could no longer foresee what lay ahead.

Since he had talked with a nitwit widow named Enola Holmes, and would tell my brother Sherlock, I needed to abandon my nearly perfect disguise.

Indeed, I needed to completely reconsider my situation.

Sighing, perched on the edge of my seat because of my bustle—or rather, luggage—I braced myself against my backwards progress. The train lurched and swayed as it rumbled along at least twice as fast as any bicycle had ever skimmed down any hill. Trees and buildings whipped past the window at a speed so tumultuous that I had to avoid looking out.

I felt a bit ill, for more than one reason.

My safe and comfortable plans for cab, hotel, genteel lodgings, and quiet waiting would no longer serve. I had been identified. Seen. Either Lestrade or my brother Sherlock would trace a young widow's steps through Belvidere and find that I had gotten onto the afternoon express train to the city. So much for misdirecting my brothers towards Wales! Although they could have no idea of my financial well-being, nevertheless, they would know now that I'd gone to London, and there was nothing I could do about it.

Except leave London as soon as I arrived, by the next train to anywhere?

But surely my brother would inquire of the ticketing agents, and now my black dress marked me. If Sherlock Holmes found that a widow had gotten on the train to, say, Houndstone, Rockingham, and Puddingsworth, he would investigate. And surely he would find me more easily in Houndstone, Rockingham, Puddingsworth, or any such place than in London.

Moreover, I *wanted* to go to London. Not that I thought Mother was there—quite the opposite, actually—but I would best be able to find her from there. And I had always dreamt of London. Palaces, fountains, cathedrals. Theatres, operas, gentlemen in tails, and ladies dripping with diamonds.

Also—and rumbling backwards towards the great city, I found myself smiling beneath my veil at this thought—the idea of hiding beneath my brothers' noses appealed all the more now that they knew. I would revise their opinion of the cranial capacity of their accidental younger sister.

Very well. London it was.

But circumstances had changed so that I could not, upon arriving in the city, take a cab. Sherlock Holmes would inquire of the cabdrivers. Therefore, I would have to walk. And night was coming on. But I could not now allow myself a hotel room. Surely my brother would inquire at all the hotels. I would have to walk for quite a distance to get myself well away from the railway station—but where to go? If I took the wrong street, I might find myself in company with someone who was not a nice sort of person. I might encounter a pickpocket, or—or perhaps even a cutthroat.

Most unpleasant.

And just as I thought this, averting my eyes from the dizzying scene outside the train's window, I glanced up instead at the glass in the corridor door.

I very nearly screamed.

There, like a full moon rising, a large face peered into the compartment.

With his nose actually pressed against the glass, the man looked in, scanning each occupant in turn. With no change in his cold expression he fixed his shadowy gaze on me. Then he turned away and moved on.

Gulping, I looked around at my fellow passengers to see whether they, too, were frightened. It appeared not. In the seat next to me, a workman in a cap sprawled snoring, his rough square-toed boots thrust out into the middle of the floor. Opposite him, a fellow in shepherd's-plaid trousers and a homburg hat studied a newspaper which, judging by etchings of jockeys and horses, concerned itself with the racetrack. And next to him, opposite me, a squat old woman fixed me with her cheery gaze.

"Something the matter, duckie?" she inquired.

Duckie? A most peculiar mode of address, but I let it pass, asking merely, "Who was that man?"

"What man, ducks?"

Either she hadn't seen him at all, or it was perfectly normal for large bald men wearing cloth caps to peer into railroad parlours, and I was being a fool.

Shaking my head dismissively, I murmured, "No harm done." Although my heart declared me a liar.

"Yer looking a bit white under all that black," my new acquaintance declared. Common, toothless crone, instead of a proper hat she wore a huge old-fashioned bonnet with a brim that flared like a fungus, tied with an orange ribbon under her bristly chin. Instead of a dress she wore a fur wrap gone half bald, a blouse somewhat less than white, an old purple skirt with new braid stuck on its faded hem. Peering at me like a robin hopeful of crumbs, she coaxed, "Yers a recent loss, duckie?"

Oh. She wanted to know about my fictitious dear departed husband. I nodded.

"And now yer bound ter London?"

Nod.

"It's the old story, isn't it, ducks?" The vulgar old woman leaned towards me with as much glee as pity. "Catched yerself a likely 'un, ye did, but now he's died"—such was the brutal word she used—"gone and died on you, he has, and left you wit'out the means to feed yerself? And ye, as yer lookin' so sick, maybe wit 'is child in yer belly?"

At first I could scarcely understand. Then, never having heard anything so unwhisperable stated out loud, and in a public place, yet, in the presence of *men* (although neither of them seemed to notice), I found myself shocked speechless. A fiery flush heated my face.

My friendly tormentor seemed to consider my blush to be affirmation. Nodding, she leaned even closer to me. "And now yer thinking ye can find yerself summat to support ye in the city? 'Ave ye ever been t'London before, m'dear?"

I managed to shake my head.

"Well, don't be makin' the old mistake, duckie, no matter what the gentlemuns promise." She leaned closer, as if telling me a great secret, yet did not lower her voice. "If ye need a few pennies to yer pocket, 'ere's the dodge: take a petticoat or two out from under yer dress—"

I truly thought I would faint. The workman, blessedly, snored on, but the other man unmistakably lifted his newspaper to hide his face.

"—won't never miss 'em," the toothless crone gabbled on. "Why, many's a woman in London hain't got a petticoat to 'er name, and ye with 'alf a dozen, I'll warrant by the puffing and the rustling of 'em."

I desperately wanted the journey and this ordeal to end, so much so that I risked a look at the window. Houses upon houses whisked past the glass now, and taller buildings, pressed together, brick to stone.

"Take 'em to Culhane's Used Clothing on Saint Tookings Lane, off Kipple Street," relentlessly continued the hag, whose squat presence now reminded me more of a toad than a robin. "Down in the East End, ye know. Ye can smell yer way there by the docks. And mind, once ye find Saint Tookings Lane, don't go to one of them other dealers, but straight to Culhane's, where ye'll get a fair sum for yer petticoats, if 'em's real silk."

The man with the newspaper rattled it and cleared his throat. Gripping the edge of my seat, I leaned away from the shocking hag as far as my bustle would allow. "Thank you," I muttered, for while I had no intention of selling my petticoats, nevertheless this dreadfully common old woman had helped me.

I had been wondering how I was to dispose of my widow's clothing and get something else. Of course, I had plenty of money to order anything I wanted, but the construction of clothing takes time. Moreover, surely my brother would inquire of the established seamstresses, and surely I would be remembered if, all clad in black, I were fitted for anything except more black, or grey with perhaps a touch of lavender or white. After the first year in mourning, that was all one was supposed to wear. Yet, given my brother's cleverness, none of that would do. I could not merely modify my appearance; I needed to transform it completely. But how? Pluck garments off of washing-lines?

Now I knew. Used clothing shops. Saint Tookings Lane, off Kipple Street. In the East End. I did
not think my brother was likely to inquire there.

Nor did I think—as I should have—that I would
risk my life, venturing there.

CHAPTER
THE
ELEVENTH

FROM MY SEAT ON THE TRAIN I CAUGHT only fleeting glimpses of London. But when I emerged from Aldersgate Station, meaning to walk briskly away, instead I stood for a moment gazing at a metropolis so dense and vast. All around me towered a man-made wilderness, buildings taller and more forbidding than any trees that ever were.

My brothers lived here?

In this—this grotesque brick-and-stone parody of any world I had ever known? With so many chimney-pots and roof-peaks looming dark against a lurid, vaporous orange sky? Lead-coloured clouds hung low while the setting sun oozed molten light between them; the Gothic towers of the city stood festive yet foreboding against that glowering sky, like candles on the Devil's birthday cake.

I stared until I grew aware of hordes of indifferent city-dwellers brushing past me, going about their business. Then I took a deep breath, closed my mouth, swallowed, and turned my back to this curiously ominous sunset.

Here in London, just as anywhere else, I told myself, the sun went down in the west. Therefore, forcing my flabbergasted limbs to move, I walked down a broad avenue leading in the opposite direction—for I wanted to go east, towards the used clothing stores, the docks, the poor streets. The East End.

Within a few blocks I walked into narrow streets shadowed by crowded buildings. Behind me the sun sank. In the city night, no stars or moon shone. But swatches of yellow light from shop windows draped the pavement, seeming to drag down the intervening darkness all the blacker, darkness out of which passersby appeared like visions, vanishing again in a few steps. Like figures out of a dream again they appeared and disappeared on the corners, where gas street-lamps cast wan skirts of light.

Or figures out of a nightmare. Rats darted in and out of the shadows, bold city rats that did not run away as I walked by. I tried not to look at them, tried to pretend they were not there. I tried not to stare at an unshaven man in a crimson cravat, a starveling boy with his clothing in rags, a great brawny man wearing a bloodied apron, a barefoot Gypsy woman on a corner—so there were Gypsies in London, too! But not the proud nomads of the country. This was a dirty beggar, all grimed like a chimney-sweep.

This was London? Where were the theatres and the carriages, the jewelled ladies in fur wraps and evening gowns, the gold-studded gentlemen in white ties and cutaway tails?

Instead, like a kind of walking doghouse, along came a pale man wearing sign-boards, front and back:

For

IRREPROACHABLE

HAIR GLOSS

Use

Van Kempt's

Oil of

Macassar

Dirty children swirled around him, taunting, knocking his dented derby off his head. A capering girl shrieked at him, "Where do ye keep the mustard?" Evidently a great joke, for her mates laughed like little banshees.

The dark streets rang with such noise, shopkeepers roaring at the street urchins, "Be off with you!" while wagons rattled past and a fishmonger cried, "Fresh haddock fer yer supper!" and sailors shouted greetings to one another. From an unswept doorway a stout woman shrieked, "Sarah! Willie!" I wondered if her children were tormenting the board-man. Meanwhile, folk brushed past me, chatting in vulgarly loud voices, and I walked faster, as if I could somehow escape.

What with so many strange sights and so much commotion, small wonder I didn't hear the footsteps following me.

I did not notice until the night deepened and darkened—or so it seemed at first, but then I realised it was the streets themselves that had grown grimmer. No more shops gave light, only glaring public houses on the corners, their drunken noise spilling into the darkness. I saw a woman standing in a doorway with her face painted, red lips, white skin, black brows, and I guessed I was witnessing a lady of the night. In her tawdry low-cut gown she reeked so badly of gin that I could smell it even above the stench of her seldom-washed body. But she was not the only source of odour; the whole East End of London stank of boiled cabbage, coal smoke, dead fish along the nearby Thames, sewage in the gutters.

And people. In the gutters.

I saw a man lying drunk or sick. I saw children huddled together like puppies to sleep, and I realised they had no homes. My heart ached; I wanted to awaken those children and give them money to buy bread and meat pies. But I made myself walk on, lengthening my stride. Uneasy. Some sense of danger —

A dark form crawled along the pavement in front of me.

Crawled. On her hands and knees. Her bare feet dragging.

I faltered to a halt, staring, struck motionless and witless by the sight of an old woman reduced to such wretchedness, with only a single torn and threadbare dress inadequately covering her, no underpinnings beneath it. Nothing on her head, either, not even so much as a rag of cloth, and no hair. Only a mass of sores covered her scalp. I choked back a cry at the sight, and dully, creeping at a snail's pace on her knuckles and her knees, she lifted her head a few inches to glance at me. I saw her eyes, pallid like gooseberries —

But I had stood still a moment too long. Heavy footsteps sounded behind me.

I leapt forward to flee, but it was too late. The footfalls rushed upon me. An iron grip grasped my arm. I started to scream, but a steely hand clamped over my mouth. Very close to my ear a deep voice growled, "If you move or cry out, I *will* kill you."

Terror froze me. Wide-eyed, staring into darkness, I couldn't move. I could barely breathe. As I stood gasping, his grip left my arm and snaked around me, clasping both arms forcibly to my sides, pressing my back against a surface that might as well have been a stone wall had I not known it to be his chest. His hand left my mouth, but within an instant, before my trembling lips could shape a sound, in the dim night I saw the glint of steel. Long. Tapering to a point like a shard of ice. A knife blade.

Dimly, also, I saw the hand that held the knife.

A large hand in a kidskin glove of some tawny colour.

"Where is he?" the man demanded, his tone most menacing.

What? Where was who? I could not speak.

"Where is Lord Tewksbury?"

It made no sense. Why would a man in London be accosting me about the noble runaway? Who could know I had been in Belvidere?

Then I remembered the face I had seen pressed against the glass, peering into the train compartment.

"I will ask you once more, and once only," he hissed. "Where is Viscount Tewksbury, Marquess of Basilwether?"

It must by then have been past midnight. Shouts blurred by ale still rang from the public houses, along with bawdy off-key singing, but the cobblestones and pavements stood empty. What I could see of them. Anything could have lurked in the shadows. And this was not the sort of place where one could hope for help.

"I—I, ah . . . ," I managed to stammer, "I have no idea."

The knife blade flashed under my chin, where, through my high collar, I could feel its pressure against my throat. Gulping, I closed my eyes.

"No games," my captor warned. "You are on your way to him. Where is he?"

"You are mistaken." I tried to speak coolly, but my voice shook. "You are labouring under some absurd delusion. I know nothing of—"

"Liar." I felt murder in his arm muscles. The knife jumped, jerked in his hand, slashing at my throat, finding instead the whalebone of my collar. With what could have been my last breath I screamed. Twisting in the cutthroat's grip, flailing, I lashed upwards and backwards with my carpet-bag, feeling it hit his face before it flew out of my grasp. He cursed fearsomely, but although his hold on me loosened, he did not let go. Shrieking, I felt his long blade stab at my side, strike my corset, then stab again, seeking a passageway to my flesh. Instead, it slit my dress, a long, ragged wound, as I tore away from him and ran.

I cried, "Help! Someone help me," blundering into darkness, running, running, I knew not where.

"In here, ma'am," said a man's voice, high and squeaky, out of the shadows.

Someone had after all heard me crying for help. Nearly sobbing with relief, I turned towards the voice, plunging down a narrow, steep alley between buildings that reeked of tar.

"This way." I felt his skinny hand take my elbow, guiding me a crooked way towards something that glimmered in the night. The river. My guide pulled me onto a narrow wooden walkway that shifted beneath my feet.

Some instinct, a misgiving, made me balk, my heart beating harder than ever.

"Where are we going?" I whispered.

"Just do as yer told." And in less time than it takes to tell it, he had twisted my arm behind my back, shoving me forward, towards I knew not what.

"Stop it!" I braced the heels of my boots against the planks, suddenly more furious than afraid. I had, after all, been mauled about, had lost my carpet-bag, had been threatened by a knife, my clothing ruined, my plans also in tatters, and now the one whom I had thought to be my rescuer seemed to be turning into a new enemy. I became wrought. "Stop, villain!" I shouted as loudly as I could.

"Hold yer tongue!"

Twisting my arm painfully, he gave a hard shove. I could not help stumbling forward, but I continued to call out. "Curses! Let go of me!"

Something heavy clouted me over my right ear. I fell sideward into darkness.

It is not fair to say that I fainted. I have never fainted and I hope I never do. Say, rather, that for some time I was knocked out of my senses.

When I blinked and opened my eyes, I found myself awkwardly half sitting, half lying on an odd sort of curved plank floor, my hands bound behind my back and my ankles similarly tied, with rough hemp cord, in front of me.

Swinging from a crude plank ceiling close overhead, an oil lamp gave off a hot, choking odour as it leaked a dim light. I saw big stones grouped around turpentine-coloured water near my feet, as if in awful travesty of my favourite dell at home. The floor seemed to move beneath me. I felt lightheaded. Closing my eyes, I waited for my sickness to pass.

But it did not pass. My sense of movement, I mean. And, I realised, I was light-headed only because my captor, whoever he was, had taken my hat away, probably for fear of its pins. My head, clad in only its own snaggled hair, felt exposed, and my world seemed to jolt and rock, but I was not ill.

I was, rather, lying in the cellar of a boat.

The hull, I mean. I remembered that was what they called it. While I had no experience of barges and ships and such, I had ridden in a rowboat a time or two, and I recognised the floating, bumping motion of a small craft in its stall, so to speak. In the water but with its head tied to a post. The ceiling where the lamp swung was the underside of a deck. The filthy puddle at my feet was called "bilge," and the stones, I believe, were "ballast."

Opening my eyes, peering into the gloom, I scanned my shadowy prison and realised that I was not alone.

From the opposite side of the hull, with his hands behind his back and his bound ankles just across the bilge from mine, a boy faced me.

Studied me.

Scowling dark eyes. Hard jaw.

Cheap, ill-fitting clothing. Bare feet that looked soft, sore, pale.

An uneven stubble of fair hair.

And a face I had seen before, although only upon the front page of a newspaper.

Viscount Tewksbury, Marquess of Basilwether.

CHAPTER
THE
TWELFTH

But—but that was absurd. Impossible. He was supposed to be running away to sea.

Quite without any proper introduction I exclaimed, "What in Heaven's name are *you* doing here?"

He arched his golden brows. "You presume an acquaintance, miss?"

"For mercy's sake, I presume nothing." Indignation and surprise spurred me to sit up straight, not without difficulty. And ill temper. "I *know* who you are, *Tewky.*"

"Don't call me that!"

"Very well, Lord Tewksburial-at-sea, what are you doing barefoot in a boat?"

"One might with equal justice ask what a snip of

a girl is doing all gadded up as a widow." Sharpening, his tone grew ever more aristocratic.

"Oh," I shot back, "a cabin boy with an Eton accent?"

"Oh. A widow with no wedding ring?"

Not being able to see my hands bound behind my back, I hadn't realised. But now, propped upright by my bustle and working my fingers against the cords that bound my wrists, I exclaimed, "What did he take my gloves for?"

"They," corrected His Lordship the Viscount. "Plural. Two of them. They wanted to steal your ring, and found none." Despite his arrogant, lecturing air, I could see how ashen his face was, could see his lips trembling as he spoke. "They went through your pockets also, finding a few shillings, some hairpins, three licorice sticks, a rather filthy handkerchief—"

"Indeed." I tried to quell this recitation, for the thought that, while I was unconscious, strange men had put their hands into my pockets—the very idea made me shudder. Thankfully, they had not actually touched my person, for my improvised wearable baggage remained where it belonged. I could feel bust enhancer, hip regulators, and dress improver occupying their positions.

"—a comb, a hairbrush, a flowery little booklet of some sort—"

My heart panged as if he had just killed my mother before my eyes. My eyes burned. But I had to bite my lip, for this was neither the time nor the place to mourn my loss.

"—and, as one side of your dress is sliced wide open, a glimpse of that scandalous pink corset you're wearing."

"Nasty boy!" My misery fueled anger. Hot with embarrassment and quivering with fury, I flared at him, "You deserve to be right where you are, bound hand and foot—"

"And how do you, dear girl no older than I, deserve the same?"

"I am older!"

"How much older?"

I almost told him before I remembered I must reveal my age to no one. Confound him, he was clever.

And, despite his bravado, frightened.

As frightened as I was.

After taking a deep breath, I asked him softly, "How long have you been imprisoned here?"

"Only an hour or so. While the little one was snatching me, it seems, the big one was following you for some reason. I—"

He broke off as heavy footsteps sounded overhead. They halted, a square of lantern light opened at the far end of our prison, and I found myself watching the rather ludicrous sight of a man appearing from the back and from the bottom up, rubber boots first, as he descended into our den by a ladder.

"No more'n an hour ago," he said to someone up above as he climbed down; I recognised his squeaky voice. Skinny, stunted, bent, this man cowered like a much-kicked and underfed mongrel. "Found him right where ye tole me in yer wire, moochin' about the docks where they berth the *Great Eastern*. We know what ter do wid 'im, but wot about the girl?"

"Much the same," growled the other man's voice as he descended in his turn. I knew that voice, too, and watched stoically as black-booted feet were followed by hulking limbs clad in dark clothing that might once have belonged to a gentleman, although now gone to seed. His pale kid gloves, I could see in the light of the lantern he bore, were yellow. Many gentry, men and ladies alike, wore kid gloves, often yellow, serving to advertise a certain social class.

When the back of the massive man's head came into view, however, I saw that he wore not a gentleman's hat, but the cloth cap of a labourer.

I was prepared, then, when he turned around and I saw his face.

It was, indeed, the cold white face that had peered like a baleful moon into my railway car compartment. Or a baleful white skull; as he removed his cap I saw that he was quite bald, disgustingly so, like a maggot, except for bristles of wiry reddish hair protruding from his ears.

"I thought ye were after 'er only in case I missed me mark," said the other.

"To make doubly sure, yes," drawled the big bald one, "but also because she says her name is Holmes." As he spoke to his companion, he watched my face with malicious enjoyment, smirking as my eyes flew open and my jaw dropped. I could not help showing my shock, for how did he know who I was? How could he possibly know?

Satisfied by my reaction, he turned back to his companion. "She says she's related to Sherlock

Holmes. If that is true, there is swag to be got for her."

"Why'd ye try to kill 'er, then?"

So this bulky man with the hair in his ears was, as I had surmised, the cutthroat who had attacked me.

He shrugged his burly shoulders. "She vexed me," he said with chill indifference.

I managed to close my gaping mouth as things began to make sense. He had been looking for me on the train. He had followed me from the station.

Yet—yet nothing made sense. Why, accosting me, had he thought I knew where Lord Tewksbury was?

"Shrew." The cutthroat looked straight at me with eyes like black ice, something—I could not think what—familiar about that glare, although I'll not deny it scared me so badly that I shook. He told me, "Girls hereabouts mostly don't have the shillings for corsets. I've sliced a few bellies wide open in my time. Don't cross me again."

I sat silent, unable to think of any suitable reply. In truth, frightened witless.

But then the other man, the rickety one, spoilt the effect by saying to his companion, "Well, ye better watch yerself and don't make Sherlock 'Olmes vexed, either. Wot I hear, ye don't fool wit' that gent."

The big one turned on him. "I fool with whomever I please." His tone menaced like a knife blade. "I'm going to sleep. You guard these two."

"That were my intention anyway," the other muttered, but only after the hulking brute had disappeared back up the ladder.

The skinny one, the mongrel watchdog, settled himself with his back against the ladder and stared at us with vicious little eyes.

I demanded of him, "Who are you?"

Even in the dim light of the oil lamp, I could see that his yellow grin lacked several teeth. "Prince Charmant der Horseapple, at yer service," he told me.

An obvious falsehood. I scowled at him.

"While we're doing introductions," said Lord Tewksbury to me, "what, pray tell, is your name?"

I shook my head at him.

"No talkin'," Squeaky Voice said.

"What," I asked him coldly, "do you and your friend intend to do with us?"

"Take ye dancin', dearies. I told ye, no talkin'!"

Unwilling to amuse this reprehensible person any longer, I lay down sideward on the bare planks, with the cut portion of my dress beneath me. I closed my eyes.

It is difficult to sleep, or even pretend to sleep, with one's hands tied behind one. To make matters worse, the tips of my steel corset ribs jabbed me painfully under the arms.

My thoughts, as well as my body, were far from comfortable. The mention of "swag" indicated money, leading me to conclude that I was being held for ransom. I could not imagine a more humiliating way to be returned to my brothers, who would no doubt then send me off to boarding school with a spanking. I wondered whether they would take my money away. I wondered how, how, *how* the big ruffian had learned of me to follow me, and, even more appalling, had learned of Viscount Tewksbury and wired his mongrel-like accomplice about him. I wondered what "much the same" meant. Quivering with terror, I urged myself to be alert for any chance to escape. Yet at the same time I knew I would be wise to breathe more calmly, stop trembling, muster my energy, try to sleep.

Because of the shape of the boat's hull, I lay on an incline somewhat hammock-shaped but far from restful, even with all the padding I wore. Shifting my limbs, I tried for a less cramped position, without success, because the steel ribs of my confounded corset now not only tormented my arms, but at the other end they poked through the rent in my dress, reminding me all too plainly of how that cutthroat's knife had—

Steel. Knife.

I lay very still.

Oh. Oh, if only I could do it.

After a moment's thought, I opened my eyes just enough to take a peek at Squeaky the Watchdog through my eyelashes. How fortunate that my modesty had made me lie upon my right side, facing him, in order to conceal my corset. He still sat with his back against the ladder, but with his head lolling. Asleep.

And why not, for as long as he remained in position by the ladder, how could we possibly get past him? But I would deal with that problem later.

As silently as I could, I turned the upper portion of my person, trying to place my bound wrists against a protruding rib of my corset.

It was not easy, as the slash in my dress was at the side. But by straining one arm to the utmost while propping myself up on the elbow of the other, clenching my teeth to keep from making a sound, I contrived to loop the cord that bound my wrists around the tip of a steel corset stay.

So twisted that I could barely move, I nevertheless managed to force back the heavily starched fabric that sheathed the steel.

Then, even more contorted, I began trying to cut through the cords.

Not once did I look at Lord Tewksbury. I tried to think of him as little as possible, and then only to assure myself he must be asleep. Otherwise, I would have felt the mortification of my posture beyond bearing.

Back and forth, back and forth, with great difficulty I sawed away with my hands and arms while pressing my bound wrists against the steel. Painfully, and for quite a long time. I cannot say how many foul hours ensued, for there was no telling night from day in that hole. There was no telling, either, whether I was making any progress against the cords, for I could not see what I was doing. I could feel that I was cutting *myself*. But I clenched my jaw and bore down all the harder, my gaze fixed on the sleeping guard, my ears straining to hear beyond my own panting breath. I felt more than heard the lapping of waves, the slopping of bilge water, the occasional muffled bump as the boat drifted against its pier —

Squeaky twitched as if pestered by a flea. I had just time to flatten myself, hands hidden from his view behind my back, before he opened his eyes.

"See 'ere," he complained, glaring at me, "what yer rockin' the bloody boat fer?"

CHAPTER
THE
THIRTEENTH

I FROZE, COWERING, LIKE A RABBIT IN a thicket.

But from the other side of the hull an imperious voice spoke. "What for? I *desire* this boat to rock. I demand, nay, I *command* this boat to rock." And rock it did, for there sat young Viscount Tewksbury, Marquess of Basilwether, leaning back to front to back again, disturbing our prison's repose.

"Ye there!" Squeaky's flinty stare turned to him. "Stop 'at."

"Make me." Haughtily Lord Tewksbury met his glare and kept rocking.

"Ye want me to *make* you?" Squeaky lurched to his feet. "Think yer a toff, do you? By jingo, I'll show ye." Fists balled, he walked over to Tewksbury, and in so doing he turned his back to me.

I sat up and twisted around, leaning to one side, fumbling again to find the corset rib with my bound hands.

With vicious force our captor kicked young Lord Tewksbury in the leg.

The boy made no sound, but I could have cried out. I wanted to strike, seize, stop that nasty man. Indeed, I lost my head entirely, struggling against the cords that bound my wrists so wildly that it seemed I would wrench my arms out of their sockets.

Then something snapped. It hurt terribly.

Squeaky kicked Tewksbury again. "Keep going," the boy said. "I like it." But his strained voice showed that he lied.

My arms hurt so badly that I thought I had broken a bone, rather than the cord, until I found myself looking at my own hands, which had presented themselves in front of my face like disreputable strangers. Battered, bloodied. Rags of hemp dripping from their wrists.

"Ye like it? I'll see ye like it," squeaked our scurvy wretch of a guard, kicking Lord Tewksbury for the third time, quite hard.

This time Tewky whimpered.

And simultaneously I rose to my feet, my ankles

still bound—but walking was not necessary, as I stood directly behind our captor. My hands, which seemed to know what to do better than I did, selected a large rock from the ballast even as Squeaky cocked his leg to kick again. Before he could do so, I hoisted my primitive weapon and brought it down with great decision upon his head.

He fell without a sound, splashed into the bilge water, and lay still.

I stood gawking at him.

"Idiot, untie my hands!" cried Lord Tewksbury.

The downed man continued as he was. Inert, but breathing.

"*Untie* me, fool!"

The boy's peremptory tone prodded me into motion. I turned my back on him.

"Ninny, what are you *doing*?"

I was preserving my scant remaining modesty, although I did not tell him so. Unbuttoning part of my bodice, I reached deep into my frontal baggage and found the penknife I had removed from my drawing kit and stowed in my "bust enhancer" along with a pencil and some folded sheets of paper. After buttoning up again, I opened the penknife, stooped, and cut the cords away from my ankles.

Unable to see these proceedings through my expanse of black skirt, Lord Tewksbury stopped giving orders and actually began to beg. "Please. Please! I saw what you were doing and I helped you, didn't I? Please, you—"

"Shhh. In a moment." Once I had freed my feet, I turned, stepped past the motionless form of our guard, then leaned over the captive boy. With one quick snick I severed the cord binding his hands behind his back. Then I handed him the knife so he could free his feet himself. On the skirt of my ruined dress I wiped the blood from my wrists. I looked at the cuts—not so deep as to be dangerous—then felt at my hair, which had fallen out of any semblance of a bun to straggle around my shoulders. Finding a few hairpins in its tangles, I tried to close the rip in my dress with them.

"*Do* come on!" urged young Viscount Tewksbury, now on his feet with my penknife, still open, gripped like a weapon in his hand.

He was right, of course; there was no time for me to make myself presentable. Nodding, I approached the ladder that led to freedom, with Lord Tewksbury at my side. As we reached it, however, we hesitated, eyeing each other.

"Ladies first?" said His Lordship uncertainly.

"I yield in favor of the gentleman," I responded, thinking only that a girl must never place herself in such a position that a male might look up her skirt. Not at all thinking of what might await us above.

Nodding, still clutching the penknife, Tewksbury climbed the ladder.

Light blinded me as he lifted the hatch. Night had passed into day, whether morning or afternoon I knew not. I retain only a vague, blinking, silhouetted impression of the cautious way the young viscount put his head forth and looked around. Quite silently he laid the hatch cover aside, climbed out, and beckoned urgently to me.

Climbing as quickly as I could, I realised he was waiting for me, his hand extended to help me out of the hold. Despite having called me in close succession an idiot, a fool, and a ninny, the boy showed traces of gallantry. He would have been wiser to flee without me. But it seemed right that, as we had been prisoners together, we would escape together. Certainly it had not occurred to me to leave him behind, and evidently he had not thought to leave me behind, either.

Reaching the top of the ladder, I grasped his hand—

An awful voice roared a curse such as I had never previously heard or imagined. As my head rose above the level of the hatch, I saw a tall, massive, scarlet form hurtle out of a cabin and across a too-brief expanse of deck towards us.

In that awful moment I learned that gentlemen, or at least a certain ungentle man, wore unmentionables made of blood-red flannel from wrist to ankle.

I screamed.

"Come *on*!" Springing to his feet, Tewksbury all but lifted me off the ladder, flinging me away from the charging red menace. "Run!"

He looked as if he intended to hold the brute off with his little penknife.

"*You* run." Hoisting a wad of skirt and petticoat above my knees with one hand, I grabbed him by the collar with the other as I fled to the far end of the boat. Together—although necessarily I let go of him—we leapt across a yard of water to the wobbly planking of what I suppose might be called a pier. Then, hauling at my skirt with both hands, I ran as fast as I could along that narrow, unsteady path.

"You won't get far!" bellowed a ferocious voice from the boat. "Just wait till I get some clothes on me and my hands on you!"

Being long of limb, I like to run, but not tripping over my own confounded clothing, and definitely not on a labyrinth of rotting green-slimed planks. A bewilderment of piers and brackish water, wharves and cat-walks, and yet more stinking water lay between us and the taverns and warehouses that rose at the edge of the Thames.

"Which — *way*?" gasped Tewky — for I could no longer think of him as lord, viscount, duke's son; he was my comrade now, panting along right behind me.

"I can't tell!"

Surrounded by tar-dark water, at a dead end, we slipped and skittered, turning to dart back. Once again an arm of water blocked our way. I began to shake, for if I fell into that black river, it would be the end for me; I would drown. I doubted whether Tewksbury could swim, either. But there was no time for dithering. At too scant a distance our massive enemy sprang out of his cabin again, with some decent covering thrown onto his person this time, roaring, "I'll kill you both!" Like a charging bear he lunged from his craft onto the labyrinthine wharf.

Even worse, a small, crooked form followed him the way a starved dog follows a beggar. Evidently I had not hit Squeaky hard enough.

"Jump!" I wailed, and with my skirts billowing I leapt for another pier.

It rocked beneath me, but I managed to keep my footing, and just as I gasped for air, it rocked again, even worse, as Tewksbury landed with a thump beside me. Lacking breath to scream outright, I squeaked like a clothesline reel. Tewky grabbed my arm, crying, "Run!" and this time he led as we fled. At some point, he had lost my penknife; his right hand trembled weaponless. My shaking redoubled, for I felt the heavy tread of the cutthroat quaking the dock beneath us.

"Oh, *no!*" I cried as we slid to a halt at the end of another pier that led nowhere.

Tewky said something unrepeatable.

"Shame on you. This way." Turning, I took the lead again, and in a few moments, at last we scrambled to firmer footing of cobbles, brick, and mortar. But our enemies, who knew their way, reached

shore just as we did, only a stone's throw behind us.
I could see the blood on Squeaky's head and the rage
in his squinty eyes. I could see the hair in the big cutthroat's ears and the wrath reddening his platter
face. Blood on the moon, an ill omen.

I confess I screamed again—indeed, I shrieked
like a shot rabbit. Blindly, with Tewky's hand in
mine, I fled up a narrow street and around a corner.
"Hurry!" Zigzagging between heavily loaded wagons drawn by straining draft horses, we ran at an
angle across the street to the next turning.

By now out of breath, moist of face and dress, all
too aware of the heat of the day, I could still hear
running footsteps following us.

Tewky was dropping behind. Dragging him
along, I could feel a wince of pain in his every stride.
His feet. Bare, sore, hitting on hard stone. And it
was all uphill, fleeing from the river.

"Come *on!*"

"Can't," the boy panted, trying to yank his hand
out of mine. I tightened my grip.

"Indeed you can. You must."

"You—go. Save yourself."

"No." Blinking away my blind panic, I looked
around me as we ran. We seemed to be reaching the

end of wagons and docks and warehouses. Now we ran along a poor street of shabby lodgings and even shabbier businesses: a fishmonger's, a pawn shop, an umbrella mender. And street vendors: "Live mussels, live oysters!" "Sweet ices here! Cold sweet strawberry ices!" There were people about, a dustman with a donkey-cart, men with barrows of scrap metal, women and girls afoot in caps and aprons that should have been white but had grimed to the colour of mushrooms. People, but not the sort likely to help us, and not enough of them so that a barefoot, fleeing boy could escape notice, let alone a breathless, dishevelled, bareheaded girl in the torn, blood-smeared dress of a widow.

"Stop, thieves!" bellowed a voice behind us, hoarse but still roaring. "Stop those two scoundrels! Villains! Pickpockets!"

Faces turned to stare at Tewky and me as we fled through a street of junk stores: secondhand furniture, used clothing, hats refurbished, shoes and boots resoled, used clothing again. Faces seemed to rise out of a haze of heat and terror, loom for a moment, then flash by.

One of the faces I knew in passing, although I could not think where I had seen it before.

Then, as we ran on, I remembered.

"Tewky! Quick!" Dodging off the street, I darted up a narrow passageway between two ramshackle boardinghouses, turned past the corner of a cow shed, and fled through the stinking mews behind the buildings, redolent of donkey, goat, goose, and hen. I turned again—

"You can't get away!" a fearsome voice roared from behind the cow shed, far too close for comfort.

"Give it up!" yelled another voice, squeaky.

"Idiot," Tewksbury cried, evidently addressing me. "Why are we going in a circle? They'll catch us!"

"You'll see. Follow me." Letting go of his hand and also of my remaining shreds of modesty, I ripped open the buttons of my upper bodice. Running down quite a filthy alley, I thrust my forearm into my frontal baggage and, my fingers encountering a packet of crisp papers, withdrew one. Hiding it in my palm as I rounded the final corner back into the street, I dashed towards a used clothing store.

The proprietor stood outside the door, enjoying the street scene and the cooling breeze. But when she saw me making towards her, her cheery expression chilled and turned to alarm. Rather than resembling a robin or a toad, she looked like a mouse under the paw of the cat. "No!" she gasped as I ran up to her. "No, Cutter would kill me. It's more than my life is worth—"

There was no time for discussion. Tewky and I had only a moment before the two villains would round the corner and sight us again. In that moment, I thrust a bank note for a hundred pounds into the hands of, presumably, Mrs. Culhane, grabbed Tewky by the sleeve, and dragged him with me into Culhane's Used Clothing Emporium.

CHAPTER
THE
FOURTEENTH

GASPING FOR BREATH, WE DARTED INTO A gloomy, dirty, cluttered room that felt as close as an oven. From one side wall hung a number of long cloaks and mantles; for quick concealment we pressed ourselves into their shadowy folds. Trembling, hands clenched, I watched the front door, waiting to see whether my bribe would succeed.

"Hide under a table!" Tewky whispered.

I shook my head. Poised to flee, staring out the front door and window, I saw how folk scattered, giving way, as the hulking cutthroat and his squeaky mongrel of a companion barrelled down the middle of the street, glaring in all directions. I saw the big ruffian grab a loiterer by the collar, almost lifting the man off his feet, shouting into his face. The poor fellow gestured in our direction.

And where Mrs. Culhane had gone, I did not know.

But there she was again, standing with her back to me; she looked like a plaid tortoise with a limp bow of apron strings across its middle.

Our moon-faced enemy and his follower strode up to her. Towered over her. Even rickety Squeaky stood taller than she did. And I'm not sure I could have braved the ferocity in their glares.

But the squat old woman occupied that doorway like a plug. I saw her shake her head. I saw her gesture towards the far end of the street.

I saw the sunlit doorway as a halo of glory surrounding her.

I saw the two villains turn away.

Hanging on to somebody's old cape for support, I sagged against the wall with relief.

Tewky folded like an easel, sinking to the floor.

Mrs. Culhane quite sensibly did not come in at once, but stood at the door for a while longer. By the time she entered, I had recovered my strength, found a back room with a water tap, soaked a rectangle of faded red flannel, and applied it to Tewky's face. When he sat up, I transferred my attention to his suffering feet. Dabbing with the rag, trying to remove dirt and blood without hurting him too much, I was studying his raw, sore soles when our toad-like saviour came in, shut and locked her shop door, drew down its blind, and waddled over to me.

"So," she said, "one day yer a grievin' widder, and the next day it turns out yer a stringy-hair girl runnin' from Cutter and Squeaky."

"Indeed? And who might the gentlemen be? We were not introduced."

"I don't doubt it. That's me stomach binder yer using fer a rag."

I stood up. "Merciful heavens, I think I've paid you for it."

She faced me unsmiling, no cheery robin chirp in her manner or voice today, no "duckie" for me. She said, "Wot ye gave me went to the neighbours. Others who saw."

This, I realised, must be partly true. She had disappeared from the doorway to bargain with bystanders for their silence.

But by the shrewd glint in her eye I knew it was also partly false. She had promised the neighbours some shillings or a few pounds at the very most.

Still, there was something honest in the grimness of her face as she told me, "There'd best be more where that came from. Cutter would slice me inside out if he knew, make no mistake about it. It's my life I'm risking fer ye."

"If you provide what we need," I told her, "there will be more."

So it was that the next day Tewky and I slipped out of her shop by the back door, strengthened and transformed. We had taken refuge in her rather slovenly kitchen—for she lived in three rooms on the first floor, over the shop—and we had accepted her lumpy porridge gratefully. We had slept, I on her foul-smelling sofa, Tewky on quilts on her floor. We had taken sponge baths. We had applied bag balm (ointment for cow udders) to Tewky's feet, then wrapped them in bandages. We had outfitted ourselves in apparel from Culhane's Used Clothing, burning our old things in the kitchen stove.

We had *not* talked, not even to tell one another our names. Our sour-faced hostess had asked us no questions, and we had offered no information. Tewky and I did not even converse between ourselves, lest she overhear. I did not trust her; I would not have put it beyond her to separate me from all of my money if she discovered where I kept it.

Therefore I never removed my clothing in her presence, and I never removed my corset at all, not even to sleep. That once-despised garment had become my most precious possession — so long as I did not actually tighten it! Its steely protection had saved my life. Its starchy structure supported and concealed the bust enhancer, dress improver, and hip regulators that disguised both me and my financial means.

I believe and hope that Mrs. Culhane — if that was indeed her name — never discovered this secret. We spoke only to conduct business: Might her shop provide a suit of clothes not too much worn for the boy, and a cap, and an ample pair of shoes, and thick socks? And for me, a blouse, and a bustled or gored skirt such as a typist or glove-counter girl might wear, made of practical material, with pockets? And a jacket, also with pockets, its hem flared to fit over the top of the skirt? And gloves not too spoilt, and a hat not too far out of fashion, and would she give me a bit of help with my hair?

I felt naked to the eyes of the world, leaving that place without my thick black widow's veil to cover my face, but the truth was that even my own brothers might not have known me. I stooped, and peered nearsightedly through "pince-nez" eyeglasses clipped onto my nose, perched there like a bizarre metal bird. Over the eyeglasses, a considerable fringe of false hair both decorated and hid my forehead, assisting the pince-nez in altering my profile. And over the hair I wore a straw hat trimmed with bits of lace and feathers, very much like any cheap straw hat worn by any struggling young woman in the city.

"Now I just need a parasol," I told Mrs. Culhane.

She gave me one dyed a hideous but stylish chemically derived green, then escorted us to her back door and held out her hand. Upon her palm I placed, as I had promised, another bank note. We exited, and she closed the door behind us without a word.

Once we had achieved the street, I shuffled as I walked, acting half blind, feeling my way with the folded parasol. I did this partly as disguise, and partly so that Tewky, whose feet were still quite sore, would not appear to struggle along, but rather to walk slowly, accompanying me, for my sake. In our clothing neither new nor worn-out, neither rich nor poor, I hoped we would escape anyone's attention, for I wanted no one bearing news of us to Cutter.

But I need not have worried. All around us, folk

went noisily about their business, taking no notice of us at all. London, that great brick-and-stone cauldron of a city, seemed always on the boil with swirling human activity. A man with a barrow cried, "Ginger beer! Fresh cold ginger beer to cool yer dusty throat!" A water-cart trundled past, followed by boys cleaning the cobbles with brooms. A delivery man pedalled by on the oddest tricycle I had ever seen, with the two wheels to the front instead of the rear, and a great box strapped to the handlebars. On a corner stood three dark-haired children singing in harmony like angels, in a language I did not know, the middle one with a crockery cup extended for my penny. Just beyond and above them, a ragged man with a paste can and brush balanced on a ladder, sticking up advertisements for shoe blacking, anti-rheumatic elastic wrappings, patent safety coffins. Men in white sack jackets and white trousers nailed a quarantine notice onto the doorway of a lodging. I wondered briefly what vile fevers and diseases wafted up from the stinking Thames, and whether I would perish of cholera or scarlet fever for having set foot on Cutter's vessel.

Cutter. Charming ruffian. In one of my pockets, along with money and various other useful items I had transferred there from my bust enhancer, I carried a list I had written in some wakeful hours during the night:

Why did Cutter search the train?

Why did he follow me?

Why did he think I knew where to find Tewky?

What did he want with Tewky?

Why did he wire Squeaky to look for Tewky on the docks?

What did he mean when he said "much the same"?

Is he in the business of kidnapping?

How did he know anything about Tewky and the Great Eastern at all?

How, indeed? I had told Inspector Lestrade. And Madame what-was-her-name, the Astral Perditorian, had overheard.

Had Inspector Lestrade told others? Perhaps, eventually, but would he not first have taken steps to confirm my information? Yet that wire must have been sent to Squeaky almost immediately.

Hmm.

Such were my thoughts as my limping escort and I walked a few blocks to a better neighborhood. Here we found a park of sorts, a patch of grass with four trees under which women trundled prams and a man with a donkey cried, "Rides, treat yer kiddies, a penny a head." Beside the park, I saw, stood a number of cabs. I would be able to hire one so my little lordship would not have to walk on his suffering feet.

So far, much on our guard, we had not spoken at all, but now that we had left Cutter's haunts behind, I turned to my companion and smiled.

"Well, Tewky," I said.

"Don't call me that."

I bristled. "Very well, Lord Tewksbury of Basilwether-or-not —" But my annoyance subsided as a thought struck me. I asked, "What do you want to be called? What name had you chosen for yourself when you ran off?"

"I—" He shook his head and turned his face away. "Never mind. It doesn't matter anymore."

"Why? What are you going to do?"

"I don't know."

"Do you still want to go to sea?"

He swivelled to stare at me. "You know everything. How do you know so much? Who are you? Are you really related to Sherlock Holmes?"

I bit my lip, for I did not feel as if it would be safe to tell him anything more of myself; already he knew too much. Luckily, at that moment a newsboy howled from the corner by the cab-stand, "Read all about it! Ransom demand for Viscount Tewksbury Basilwether!"

"What?" I exclaimed. "That's preposterous!" Almost forgetting to peer and shuffle, I scuttled over and bought a newspaper.

SENSATIONAL DEVELOPMENT IN
KIDNAPPING CASE

read the headline over, once again, Tewky's portrait *à la* Little Lord Fauntleroy.

Sitting next to me on a park bench so that we

could both see the newspaper at once, Tewky made a muffled sound of dismay. "My *picture*?"

"The whole world has viewed it," I told him with, I admit, some degree of zest. Then, as he did not immediately reply, I glanced at him to see upon his face an expression of fiery red, utterly anguished humiliation.

"I can't go back," he said. "I'll never go back."

No longer gleeful, I asked, "But what if someone recognises the picture? Mrs. Culhane, for instance?"

"*She?* When ever would she look at a newspaper? She can't read. In those slums nobody can read. Did you see any newsboys at the docks?"

He was right, of course, but rather than admit it, I devoted my attention to the text of the article:

A most surprising turn of events took place this morning with the arrival of an unsigned ransom demand at Basilwether Hall, Belvidere, scene of the recent disappearance of Viscount Tewksbury, Marquess of Basilwether. Despite Chief Inspector Lestrade's most astute discovery of the young lord's cache of nautical paraphernalia in a treetop hideaway—

"Oh, no," Tewky whispered, anguished anew. Wincing, I read on without comment.

—and his subsequent energetic inquiries at the London docks, where he located several eyewitnesses who claimed to have seen the missing youngster upon the very day of his disappearance—

Which was, I realised, just one day after that of my own disappearance. So much had happened since, it was hard to believe that only three days ago, I had left Ferndell Hall.

—it would now appear that the Viscount, heir to the Basilwether title and fortune, has indeed been kidnapped. Delivered in the morning post, a brief missive pasted together out of letters cut from periodicals demanded a large sum, the amount of which the family desires to remain undisclosed. Lacking any proof that Lord Tewksbury has indeed fallen into the hands of this unknown individual or individuals, the authorities advise against paying the ransom. Famed Medium and Astral Perditorian Madame Laelia Sibyl de Papaver, however, called in by the Basilwether family at the onset of the cri-

sis, advises most strongly that the ransom, which is to be gathered in the form of gold sovereigns and guineas pending instructions for delivery, should be paid, as her communications with spiritual manifestations advise her that Viscount Tewksbury is indeed held captive and in danger of his very life unless the kidnappers receive the full cooperation of his family. Madame Laelia . . .

There was more, but at this point I ceased reading. Instead, I sat staring at — at the cab-stand, really. That was what stood before Tewky and me: sporty hansom cabs and clumsy but more roomy four-wheelers, glossy horses and scrawny horses swishing their tails while munching on nosebags of oats, portly cabdrivers and shabby cabdrivers loitering, waiting for fares. But I was not in fact seeing any of this. I was trying to remember what Madame Laelia had looked like, but so much had happened in the past three days that I retained only an impression of red hair, large face, large body, large hands in yellow kid gloves —

A small voice said, "I have to go back."

It took me a moment to turn and focus on Tewky, pale and handsome and very young, returning my gaze.

"I have to go home," he said. "I can't let those bloody villains steal from my family."

I nodded. "You have an idea who sent the ransom note, then."

"Yes."

"And you imagine, as I do, that they are still upon the hunt for you."

"For both of us. Yes, indeed."

"We'd better go to the police."

"I suppose so." But his glance slid away.

He studied the tips of his new shoes—new only in a sense, as they had all too clearly been cobbled together from pieces of leather scavenged from old boots.

I waited.

Finally he said, "It wasn't what I expected, anyway. The shipyards, I mean. The water is filthy. So are the people. They don't like one if one tries to stay clean. They think one is a snob. Even the beggars spit on one. Somebody stole my money, my boots, even my stockings. Some people are so mean, they would even steal from the crawlers."

"The crawlers?"

"Dosses, they call them, because they're always dozing. I've never seen any persons so wretched."

His voice lowered. "Old women with nothing left, not even strength to stand on their feet. They sit on the workhouse steps, half asleep but with nowhere to lay their heads, too nearly dead even to beg. And if someone gives them a penny to buy tea, they crawl away to get it."

With a shock to my heart I remembered the hairless old woman I had seen crawling on the pavement, her head all sores.

"And then they crawl back again," Tewky said, his voice lower and more struggling by the moment. "And there they sit. Three times a month they are allowed a meal and a night's sleep in the workhouse. Three times. If they ask for more than that, they are locked up and given three days at hard labour."

"*What?* But I thought the workhouse was supposed to *help* the unfortunate."

"I thought that, too. I went there to ask for shoes, and they . . . they laughed at me and hit me with a stick. Drove me away. And then . . . that nasty man . . ."

His memories of Squeaky made his eyes water. He ceased speaking.

"I'm glad you've decided to go home," I said after

a moment. "Your mother will be overjoyed to see you. She's been crying, you know."

He nodded, accepting without question that I would know this, as I seemed to know everything else.

"I'm sure you'll be able to make her understand you can't wear those Lord Fauntleroy clothes anymore."

He said very softly, "Whatever kind of clothes, it doesn't matter. I never knew . . ."

He didn't finish. But I believe he was still thinking about the dosses, poor half-alive old women who crawled. Or perhaps about bare, sore feet, and the waterfront, and Squeaky, and being kicked like a dog.

Two days in London had made me aware, too, of much that I had not known before.

And now that I did know, my own ill fortunes seemed small enough.

I stood up and hailed a cab. An open, hansom cab; I wanted us to go in style. Tewky gave me his hand like a gentleman as I climbed in, as I directed the driver, "To Scotland Yard."

CHAPTER
THE
FIFTEENTH

QUITE ASIDE FROM ACCOMPANYING TEWKY, I had my own errand at Scotland Yard.

"This is lovely!" exclaimed Tewksbury, scanning London from the hansom cab as the horse trotted along, harness jingling, directly in front of us.

I paid attention only to my own thoughts: Something needed to be done about Cutter and Madame Laelia Sibyl de Papaver, Astral Perditorian. I had no proof, but the more I turned matters over in my mind, the more I considered they might be involved in a kidnapping ring together. Inference: She had told him about me. Who else could have done so? The lodge-keeper, the duchess, her maids? Most unlikely. Of all those whom I had encountered at Basilwether Hall, only Inspector Lestrade and Madame Laelia had heard me describe the whereabouts of Lord Tewksbury. One of those two had contacted Cutter to have him wire Squeaky to take Tewky prisoner. Surely it had not been Lestrade. Conclusion: It must have been Madame Laelia.

Tewky said, "I never understood why they put the driver way up top in back, so far from the horse. Now I see. It is so that nothing obstructs one's view."

"Mmm-hmm," I murmured, continuing my dark thoughts of Madame Laelia. While appearing to be on the side of the angels, the woman had actually allied herself with the devils: Cutter and Squeaky. They kidnapped a victim, I conjectured, and then Madame Laelia was called in for her dubious services, so that while Cutter and Squeaky collected ransom, Madame Laelia was paid handsomely for her spiritual insights into the missing person's whereabouts. They all profited, and they were all in their foul business together. In Tewky's case, although initially he had run away, Cutter and Squeaky had seized the opportunity to kidnap him afterward.

While unsure how to notify the authorities without putting myself in jeopardy, I knew I had to do something to put a stop to this villainy.

Tewky said, "How pleasant it is to feel the wind in one's face on a hot day."

Annoying boy, must he chatter like a magpie? Without replying, lips pressed together, I reached into a skirt pocket and pulled out a pencil and a folded piece of paper. Hastily and rather angrily, laying the paper in my lap, I sketched an exaggerated portrait of a man. When Tewky saw what I was doing, he ceased his chitchat to stare.

"That's Cutter," he said.

Without comment I finished the likeness.

"That *is* Cutter, right down to the hair in his ears. You astonish me. How do you draw like that?"

Without answering, I turned over the folded paper, and on the fresh surface I sketched another person. Because I found myself in the proper frame of mind, wrought and energetic, I was able to do so without hesitation, without conscious memory, without thought, the pencil strokes coming swiftly to hand from some source deep within my mind.

"Who's that?" Tewky asked.

Again, I did not answer. Finishing the portrait of a large, imposing woman, I unfolded the paper and looked at both sketches at once. The caricature man and the caricature woman stood side by side.

At that moment I knew.

Of course. To be a woman, all that was necessary was to put on false hair, various Patent Amplifiers, Enhancers, Improvers, and Regulators, and the necessary concealments: dress, hat, gloves. I of all people should know.

Tewky saw, too. He whispered, "It's the same person."

The bright red wig, I thought, to hide the hairy ears and distract attention from the face. And some enhancement of the lips, eyelashes, and eyes, easy enough—face paint. No respectable lady would ever admit to the use of such artifice, but I had heard it was done. Not that this person was either respectable or a lady.

Tewky demanded, pointing from one drawing to the other, "If that's Cutter, then who is *that*?"

I told him, although the name meant nothing to him: "Madame Laelia Sibyl de Papaver."

"I don't care if yer the Prince of Wales," said the sergeant at the desk without so much as lifting his eyes to take a look at us, "ye'll wait yer turn like everybody else. Have a seat." His gaze still on his papers and blotter, he flapped a meaty hand towards the hallway behind him.

I smiled at Tewky, who, having just introduced himself as Viscount Tewksbury Basilwether, seemed inclined either to laugh or cry. "I'll wait with you," I whispered.

And somehow in the course of our visit to Scotland Yard I would accomplish my own business there. As when I had ridden my bicycle away from Kineford, my best plan now seemed not to plan.

Tewky and I sat on one of many benches ranged along the dark wood-paneled passageway, benches of a singularly adamant uprightness and rigidity, worse than any church pews I had ever experienced. Perched beside me, Tewky muttered, "You're lucky with all that padding."

What a shocking thing to say. "Hush!"

"Don't tell me to hush. Tell me who you are."

"No." I kept my voice down, for all along the passageway on other benches sat people waiting to speak with the police. Intent on their own conversations and problems, however, none of them had given us a second glance.

Tewky had the sense to lower his voice. "But you've saved my life, maybe. Or at least my honour. And you—you've done so much for me. I want to thank you. Who are you?"

I shook my head.

"Why do you want to look like an old maid?"

"Shocking boy, do mind your tongue."

"Shocking girl, am I never to learn your name?"

"Shhh!" No, I hoped not, but I did not say so. Instead, I said "Hush!" again, gripping his arm, for just down the passageway from us a door was opening, and I saw a familiar man stepping out.

Two familiar men.

For a moment I truly felt as if I might faint, and not due to any corseting, either.

Heaven help me.

One of the men was Inspector Lestrade. But I had realised, deciding to accompany Tewky into Scotland Yard, that I might encounter Lestrade, and I felt sure he would not recognise me as the black-veiled widow he had met briefly at Basil-wether Hall.

No, what made me weak with alarm was the sight of the other man: Sherlock Holmes.

Mentally I willed myself to keep breathing, to sit

naturally, to blend in with the dark woodwork and the hard bench and the framed etchings on the walls the way a hen partridge blends in with brush. *Please, they must not notice me.* If either of them recognised me, my few days of freedom were over.

Slowly they paced towards us, deep in conversation, even though my brother stood so much taller than the ferret-like Lestrade that he had to stoop to put his head close to the lesser man's. After my first startled look at them, I turned my eyes to my lap, let go of Tewky, and hid my clenched, quivering hands in the folds of my skirt.

". . . can't make head nor tail of this Basilwether case," came Lestrade's strident voice. "I do wish you would have a look at it, Holmes."

"Holmes?" gasped Tewky, sitting bolt upright at my side. "Is that *him*? The famous detective?"

I whispered, "Do please hush."

I am sure he heard strong emotion in my voice, for he actually obeyed.

Sherlock was saying to Lestrade, "Not nearly as fervidly as I wish you would assign more officers to finding my *sister*." My brother's voice, while well in tune, sounded as taut as a violin string. Something in his voice, something unspoken, made a butterfly of emotion flutter painfully in my heart.

"I would like to, my dear fellow." Sympathy in Lestrade's voice, but also a note, I thought, of gloating. "However, if you cannot give me more to work with . . ."

"The butler confirms that Mother has had no portraits taken of herself or Enola for ten years or more. Confound the woman."

"Well, we have that sketch your sister drew of her." Unmistakably I heard a glint of glee in the Scotland Yard inspector's voice.

My brother's hand shot out and caught him by the arm, halting him; the two of them stood directly in front of Tewky and me. Thanks perhaps to providence, perhaps to blind luck, Sherlock stood with his back to me.

"Look here, Lestrade." My brother did not sound angry, not exactly, but his tone, nearly hypnotic in its intensity, made my heart swell with admiration for him and commanded the other man's fullest attention. Sherlock told him, "I know you think it's a great blow to my pride, that both my mother and my sister have gone missing, I cannot find a trace of the former, and I have you to thank for information of the latter. But—"

"I assure you," Lestrade interrupted, blinking, his gaze sliding to one side, "I have thought nothing of the sort."

"Bosh. I am not blaming you for being no worse than your betters." Brushing aside that perplexing statement with one black-gloved hand, Sherlock riveted the inspector anew with his gaze. "But Lestrade, I want you to understand: You may cross Lady Eudoria Vernet Holmes off your list. She knew what she was doing, and if she has come in harm's way, she has only herself to blame."

Pain roused in my heart again, not a butterfly ache, but pain of a different sort. At the time, I did not know of my brilliant brother's one crippling weakness; I did not understand how melancholia might make him utter such harsh words.

"However, Enola Holmes is a different matter entirely," Sherlock was saying. "My sister is an innocent. Neglected, uneducated, unsophisticated, a dreamer. I feel much at fault for not staying on with her, instead of leaving her to the care of my brother, Mycroft. Despite his fine mind, he has no patience.

He never could understand that it takes time, not just harness, to train a colt. Of course the girl bolted, having more spirit than intelligence."

Underneath my false bangs and pince-nez, I scowled.

"She seemed intelligent enough when I spoke with her," said Lestrade. "She certainly deceived me. I would have sworn she was twenty-five, at least. Poised, well-spoken, thoughtful—"

My scowl smoothed away. I quite approved of Lestrade.

My brother stated, "Thoughtful and imaginative, perhaps, but certainly no stranger to the weakness, the irrationality, of her sex. Why, for instance, did she tell the lodge-keeper her name?"

"Perhaps out of sheer daring, to get in. She was sensible enough, afterward, to take herself straight away to London, where it will be very difficult to find her."

"Where anything could be happening to her, even if she *were* twenty-five. And she is only fourteen."

"Where, as I was saying earlier, anything could be happening to a young person of yet more tender years: the Duke of Basilwether's son."

At which moment Tewky cleared his throat, said, "Ahem," and stood up.

So, you see, I had no chance to think and, it seemed to me at the time, no choice.

I fled.

As the inspector and the great detective turned to gawk at the commonly clad boy, as they blinked and stared, as recognition dawned, I stood up and walked quietly away. I caught only a glimpse of my brother's face, and had I known how rare a treat it was to see Sherlock Holmes so astonished, I would have enjoyed the moment more. But I did not linger, just took a few steps down the hallway, opened the first door that presented itself, and went in, closing the door softly behind me.

I found myself in an office with several desks, all of them empty but one. "Excuse me," I said to the young constable who raised his head from his paperwork, "the sergeant wants you at the front desk."

In all likelihood assuming I was recently employed at the Yard as a shorthand transcriber or something of the sort, he nodded, got up, and went out.

I went out also, by the window. Lifting the sash, I hopped over the sill as if mounting a bicycle, alighting on the pavement as if getting off the other side. There were people passing, of course, but without a glance at any of them, as if it were perfectly normal to exit a public building in this manner, I removed my pince-nez and tossed it into the street, where a large horse promptly trod upon it. Standing straight, I walked away briskly, as befit a young professional woman. At the corner, an omnibus was just stopping. I got on, paid my fare, took a seat among many other Londoners upon the roof, and did not look back. Likely my brother and Lestrade were still questioning Tewky as the big bus trundled me away.

However, I knew it would not take them long to pick up my scent. Tewky would tell them how he and a girl dressed like a widow had escaped Cutter's boat together. A girl named Holmes. Probably by now Tewky had turned to me, wanting to introduce me, but finding nothing except two sketches — I hoped Lestrade, after talking with Tewky, might realise the significance of the sketches — two caricatures lying on the bench along with a hideous green parasol.

I rather regretted having to leave Tewky so abruptly, without a farewell.

But it could not be helped. I had to find Mum.

I also very much regretted not having been able to spend more time with my brother Sherlock, even if only in disguise, to look at him, listen to him, admire him. I actually missed him, with yearning in my heart as if I were a ladybird, ladybird, and I wanted to fly away home—

But my famous detective brother did *not* care to find Mum. Confound him. All my fluttering feelings about him folded their wings and settled into heartache.

Although—perhaps it was just as well. Sherlock and Mycroft would have wanted Mum back in Ferndell Hall, but obviously she did not wish to be there. When—not if, but *when* I found her, I would ask of her nothing that might make her unhappy. I was not seeking her in order to take away her freedom.

I just wanted to have a mum.

That was all.

To be in communication with her. Maybe meet now and then to chat over a cup of tea.

To know where she was.

Although one could not help fearing, at the back of one's mind, that she had come to harm—still, I imagined it more likely that Mum had taken herself someplace where there were no corsets, no bustles, and perhaps no hats or boots. Someplace amid flowers and greenery. Ironic, I thought, that I, following her example and making my escape, had gone instead to this cesspool of a city where I had not yet seen a palace, a golden carriage, or a lady in ermine and diamonds. Where I had seen instead an old woman crawling on the pavement, her head infested with ringworm.

Certainly Mum could never fall to such depths. Could she?

I must be sure not; and I had only a few hours in which to act before the entire London constabulary would be alerted to look for me.

Alighting from the omnibus at the next stop, I walked a block, then hailed a cab. A four-wheeler this time, for the sake of being closed in, my face unseen. "Fleet Street," I told the driver.

As he manoeuvred through the heavy traffic of the city, I once more took paper and pencil in hand, composing a message:

THANK YOU MY CHRYSANTHEMUM ARE YOU BLOOMING? SEND IRIS PLEASE.

I distinctly remembered from *The Meanings of Flowers* that the iris indicated "a message." Irises in a bouquet alerted the receiver to pay attention to the meanings of the other flowers. The Greek goddess Iris had carried messages between Mount Olympus and Earth via the bridge of the rainbow.

Many of the other entries in *The Meanings of Flowers,* however, I could not recall so clearly. As soon as I had found lodgings, I must be sure to obtain a copy of the book for reference.

Bitterly I regretted the loss of that other, irreplaceable book my mother had given me, my most precious memento of her, my book of ciphers. What Cutter had done with it, I would never know.

(Or so I thought at the time.)

But, I assured myself, I did not need it for any practical purpose.

(Again, so I thought.)

Taking the message I had composed, I reversed it:

ESAELPSIRIDNES?GNIMOOLBUOYERAM
UMEHTNASYRHCYMUOYKNAHT

Then I zigzagged it up and down into two lines, thus:

EALSRDE?NMOBOEAUETAYHYUYNH
SEPIINSGIOLUYRMMHNSRCMOKAT

Then, swaying on my seat as my cab rumbled along, I reversed the order of the lines to compose my message. This I would place in the personal advertisements columns of the *Pall Mall Gazette*, which my mother seldom missed, plus the *Magazine of Modern Womanhood*, the *Journal of Dress Reform*, and other publications she favoured. My cipher ran as follows:

"Tails ivy SEPIINSGIOLUYRMMHNSR-CMOKAT tips ivy EALSRDE?NMOBOEAUE-TAYHYUYNH your Ivy"

I knew that my mother, who could not resist a cipher, would give this one her fullest attention if and when she saw it.

I also knew that, unfortunately, my brother Sherlock, who habitually read what he called the "agony columns" of the daily newspapers, would also notice it.

But, as he knew nothing of the way ivy runs backwards on a picket fence, perhaps he would not decipher it.

And even if he did solve it, I doubted he would understand it or connect it to me.

Once upon a time—it seemed long ago, in another world, but it was really only six weeks ago— once, pedalling along a country road and thinking of my brother, I had made a mental list of my talents, comparing them unfavorably with his.

Now, riding in a London cab instead of on a bicycle, I found myself compiling in my mind a different list of my talents and abilities. I knew things Sherlock Holmes failed even to imagine. Whereas he had overlooked the significance of my mother's bustle (baggage) and her tall hat (in which I suspected she had carried quite a stout roll of bank notes), I, on the other hand, understood the structures and uses of ladies' underpinnings and adornments. I had shown myself adept at disguise. I knew the encoded meanings of flowers. In fact, while Sherlock Holmes dismissed "the fair sex" as irrational and insignificant, I knew of matters his "logical" mind could never grasp. I knew an entire world of communications belonging to women, secret codes of hat brims and rebellion, handkerchiefs and subterfuge, feather fans and covert defiance, sealing-wax and messages in the positioning of a postage-stamp, calling cards and a cloak of ladylike conspiracy in which I could wrap myself. I expected that without much difficulty I could incorporate weaponry as well as defense and supplies into a corset. I could go places and accomplish things Sherlock Holmes could never understand or imagine, much less do.

And I planned to.

LONDON, NOVEMBER, 1888

ALL DRESSED IN BLACK, THE NAMELESS stranger emerges from her lodgings late at night to prowl the streets of the East End. From her unfashionably straight waist swings a rosary, its ebony beads clicking as she walks. The veiled habit of a nun covers her tall, thin body from head to toe. In her arms she carries food, blankets, and clothing for the poor old women who huddle on the steps of the workhouse, the crawling women called dosses, and any others whom she may find in need. The street folk accept her kindness and call her Sister. No one knows her by any other name, for she never speaks. Seemingly she has taken a vow of silence and solitude. Or perhaps she wishes not to flaunt cultivated speech, not to be betrayed by an upper-class accent.

Silent, she comes, she goes, an object of curiosity at first but after a few days scarcely noticed.

In a much wealthier and somewhat bohemian section of the city, someone is opening an office in the same Gothic residence where Madame Laelia Sibyl de Papaver, Astral Perditorian, held séances before her—or rather, his—shocking arrest, the scandal of the season. With the previous occupant gone to prison, in the house's bay window a placard has appeared: Soon to Be Available for Consultation, Dr. Leslie T. Ragostin, Scientific Perditorian. A scientist must of course be a man, and an important one, quite busy at the University or the British Museum; undoubtedly this is why no one in the well-to-do neighbourhood has yet seen the great Dr. Leslie T. Ragostin. But every day his secretary comes and goes, putting things to rights in his new office, tending to his affairs. She is a plain young woman, unremarkable except for her efficiency, very much like thousands of other young women typists and bookkeepers surviving in London so as to send a little money home to their families. Her name is Ivy Meshle.

Daily, as befits a virtuous and modest young

woman alone in the big city, Ivy Meshle lunches at the Professional Women's Tea-Room nearest to her place of employment. There, protected from any contact with the predatory male of the species, she sits alone reading the *Pall Mall Gazette* and various other periodicals. Already she has found in one of these publications a personal advertisement that interests her exceedingly, so much so that she has clipped it out and carries it on her person. It says:

"Iris tipstails to Ivy

ABOMNITEUNTNYHYATEUASRMLNRSML
OIGNHSNOOLCRSNHMMLOABIGOE"

Sometimes, alone in her cheap lodgings, Miss Meshle (or perhaps the mute, nameless Sister) draws this slip of paper from a pocket and sits down to look at it, even though she has long since deciphered it:

AM BLOOMING IN THE SUN. NOT ONLY
CHRYSANTHEMUM, ALSO
RAMBLING ROSE

This message was sent, she believes, by a contented woman who is wandering, free, in a place where there are no hairpins, no corsets, no dress improvers: with the Gypsies on the moors.

If she had any distance to travel, why did she not use the bicycle?
Why did she not leave by the gate?
If she struck out across country, on foot, where was she going?

One hypothesis answers all three questions: The runaway woman had no great distance to travel, needing only to walk out upon the countryside until she met, very likely by prearrangement, with a caravan of England's nomads.

In *The Meanings of Flowers*, the rambling rose refers to "a free, wandering, Gypsy type of life."

And if there is a touch of larceny in the nature of Gypsies, well, so there appeared to be also in Eudoria Vernet Holmes. As was demonstrated by her dealings with Mycroft Holmes. Very likely she is quite enjoying herself.

One question remains unanswered:

Why did Mum not take me with her?

Not as troublesome a thought as it used to be. That freedom-loving lady, growing old, having probably only a brief time to fulfill a dream before she dies, has done the best she can for her late-in-life daughter. Sometime—plans the girl who walks alone—perhaps in the spring, when the weather has warmed enough to permit travel, she will set out to seek for her mother among the Gypsies.

But meanwhile, as she looks at the newspaper clipping, her rather long and angular face softens, rendered almost beautiful, by a smile: for she knows that in the secret code of flowers, a rose of any sort signifies love.

END

CIPHER SOLUTION

"TIPSTAILS" INDICATES HOW THE CIPHER IS set up.

To solve, divide the cipher in half:

ABOMNITEUNTNYHYATEUASRMLNRS
MLOIGNHSNOOLCRSNHMMLOABIGOE

The first line of letters is "ivy tips," the second line "ivy tails." Following the letters up and down between lines:

AMBLOOMINGINTHESUNNOTONLYCHR
YSANTHEMUMALSORAMBLINGROSE

Then, separating the result into words:

AM BLOOMING IN THE SUN NOT ONLY
CHRYSANTHEMUM ALSO
RAMBLING ROSE

Contents

Bread Recipes